RETURN TICKET

RETURN TICKET

LYNNE
THOMPSON

CROSSWAY BOOKS

CROSSWAY BOOKS
38 De Montfort Street, Leicester LE1 7GP, England

First published 1997

British Library Cataloguing in Publication Data
A catalogue record for this book is available from the British Library.

ISBN 1-85684-159–6

Set in Garamond No. 3

Typeset in Great Britain by Parker Typesetting Service, Leicester

Printed in Great Britain by Cox and Wyman Ltd, Reading

For motherless children

near and far

ONE

She reached out a hand to touch the tawny bricks but felt no warm welcome.

The overgrown creeper crouched mute against the walls in the pale late September sun. The porch was grey with dust. As she turned the key in the lock, the cottage seemed to sigh as it breathed in the outside world.

It was much as she expected, yet without the joy.

Her eyes searched, arrested here and there by signs of the passage of time – chipped tiles round the fireplace, a grubby patch by the light switch, the sofa sagging. The odour of disturbed damp hessian wafted up from her ankles and she suppressed a sneeze.

A honey of a honeymoon cottage. And now revisited. To be restored – and to make restoration.

Slowly that afternoon, she unearthed small treasures that made living in the neglected home a more optimistic prospect. From the kitchen cupboards: a kettle, a blackened frying-pan, two battered saucepans, a few mugs, a tea-towel featuring faded sketches of local

Oxfordshire beauty spots, a pile of plates and two casserole dishes. She was cheered to find that the bike shed in the tiny overgrown garden held a stepladder, a bucket, and even a few tools. Electricity and gas supplies had been switched on, in accordance with her letter. The phone line was live and the boiler produced hot water satisfactorily. From the boot of the Metro, she fetched two suitcases and the survival kit of basic foodstuffs hastily assembled at the motorway services supermarket *en route* from Heathrow. Later, sipping scalding tea at the familiar applewood table, she reached for her notebook and pencilled several lists.

Change of address cards. Should she get some printed? Alexandra Davis is back.

She'd resisted the backward step, but now had given in, returning to the only place possible. No. Forget the cards. Perhaps they would all know, the same as they all knew what had happened at Chinese New Year. Quite likely the report of her return had rolled westwards over the oceans, circulated in gossip titbits over tea and biscuits, on street corners, returned with small change over the Post Office counter. Was it a mistake not to run to fresher fields?

Alex imagined a reluctant affection glowing from the walls in the dim lamplight. She loved this place, though fearful now of shadows from the past. And perhaps it was too soon to meet the past head-on.

She felt vulnerable. A familiar enough sensation. On impulse she visited each room in turn – the front room with its bay window darkened by overgrown shrubs, the sitting-room with the cramped tiled fireplace, the add-on kitchen and bathroom, the two dusty bedrooms reached by the pretty turning staircase and narrow landing – laying hands of blessing on the walls, praying, calling on Jehovah

8

Shammah. The Lord who is there. The simple act made her feel safer and stronger.

The truth was, these past few years Alex had lived between so many different walls that sometimes, waking suddenly in blackness, she would fight within herself to know where she was and then wait for the confirmation of shadows materializing in the gloom. Tonight, too tired to be rational, she felt suffocated in the sleeping-bag and musty blankets on the narrow single bed in the back bedroom. She slept uneasily with the lamp on, stirring into consciousness once or twice to find tears on her cheeks.

The morning was grey. Plunging her lists deep into her raincoat pocket, Alex drove off along the tree-lined lane towards Swindon. Driving was a novelty and needed all her concentration. She was relieved to discover a new DIY hypermarket on the rim of town which excused her from struggling to recall how to negotiate the route to the town centre. Soon she was striding briskly along the aisles, checking off items as she went. She glanced at her face in a display of bathroom mirrors. The face was pale, blue eyes solemn but composed above the collar of the beige raincoat. She felt her business-like exterior was convincing.

At least the decision about the colour scheme had already been made. She reached into her shoulder bag for the sample of material from the curtains she'd had made in Hong Kong, and a warm rush of remembered conversations spilled out with the snippet of cloth.

'This is perfect! Just the right country-cottage colours. Those big green and bronze leaves. Kind of old-fashioned but fresh. What do you think? It's hardly any more expensive than the blue we liked at the last shop.'

'You're right. Let's go for it! Besides, my feet are aching.

I can't remember. Did we decide on making the front room or the back sitting-room into a makeshift office?'

'Front room. We'll put a desk in the bay window. And we *won't* call it an office! Too, too *official* by far!' She laughed. 'We're taking this little house upmarket. It's the *study*, remember?'

Making plans. It had been fun to play house after five years of cheap rented apartments.

Rich cream for the walls throughout, then, just as they agreed. And a deep blue-green jade for the paintwork in both sitting-room and study. Alex spent time carefully matching the shade against her precious scrap of cotton curtain. She ticked her way down the list. Scraper, brushes, giant tins of emulsion, rolls of embossed Anaglypta paper, packets of paste, and sheets of sandpaper grated together in the trolley.

Back at the cottage, she made a hasty snack of soup and a cheese sandwich, changed into jeans and put on over her jumper an old shirt of Peter's she'd found tumbled in with the blankets in the cupboard in the back bedroom. She fixed her hair under a scarf. It was important to make a start. She set to work energetically, stripping the sitting-room walls of their faded paper roses.

Strange that both her earliest and her most horrifying recent memories should be of walls.

Suddenly she was back in the hallway of that long-ago terraced house in Northwood Grove. A journey of decades that took a split second in the memory. It was dim, lit only through an oblong of coloured glass diamonds high in the front door. Here the walls were dark brown and glossy below the middle ridge, chipped ivory above. She knew instinctively whenever she visited this memory that this was where the high and heavy pram was always parked, cornered by walls and door and stairs. Safe and undisturbed, since the front door was never used. All life burst into the house from the back, through the greasy kitchen and into the room with the big black fireplace around which crowded bodies large and small, the broadest one hung with a gaping waistcoat.

The vision of this, her grandparents' house where she lived her earliest years, was so vivid she could sometimes persuade herself it was a dream or a film set conjured up by her imagination. And what did it matter if it wasn't real? She climbed the stairs, entering the cramped room with its high brass bedstead and painted washstand, the room where she'd been cradled in a baker's wicker basket. She was the surprise offspring of a soldier, intoxicated with leave, and a bread-shop assistant whose mother had been too genteel to warn her that it was possible to be too accommodating.

The walls of Northwood Grove tumbled long ago. The whole area was condemned, flattened and replaced by more slums, this time reaching into the sky. But they were the first walls she remembered.

On with the job in hand. Alex wiped her arm across her eyes, noticing for the first time an old stain on the shirt cuff. Ink? Or motorcycle oil? She stroked it pensively.

It was only when you got close up like this, perched on the aluminium steps, soaking through the layers of paper with a cloth dripping with soapy water, that you noticed how walls had character and inconsistencies. Alternately rubbing with the cloth and scraping until the faded paper gave way in tendrils, Alex entered a new familiarity with the walls of her honeymoon cottage. She explored with her hands like a blind man, fingering here a swelling of old plaster, there the rough patch of a forgotten repair, a peppering of nail pricks, a branching hairline crack above the window. Once or twice the well-rehearsed image of another wall, a terrifying grey stone wall, flashed unbidden to her mind, but, steeling herself, she dismissed it.

Reaching up over the cottage fireplace, Alex started stripping a dark shadow, large and square, marking the position of a picture, long gone.

When she was a child, in another house, there was always a mirror hanging over the fireplace. Yes, that too was a scene to which she was transported easily.

'That's enough preening and fancyin' yerself in the mirror, madam. Get away from that fireplace. Yer blockin' the heat!'

She backed away nervously. Had Dad spotted the faint trace of pink lipstick, rather inexpertly drawn? She slipped her feet into her shoes, wriggled straight the denim skirt, feeling surreptitiously to see if the broken suspender was holding, grabbed the cardigan from the back of the settee.

'I'm going to be late, Dad. Must run. Bye.'

'And talkin' of late, you be in on time tonight, my girl. You might be sixteen today but sixteen's still only a babbie and don't you forget it. You know I worries if yer out past ten.'

Resentment rising, she slammed the door behind her in futile protest and ran to the bus stop on the common. Ran like the wind, forgetful of the little pointy heels on her birthday brown shoes, uncaring of the skirt wrinkling up her thighs. Eyes already seeing the smoke-filled snooker room at the social club and the boy lounging by the one-armed bandit. Not a backward glance for the scene engraved without affection in her mind. She'd lived at 69 Stonebridge Road for an eternity. The estate was a maze of copies – khaki sandblasted fronts, front doors in one of three colours, with matching coalshed doors. Identical metal gates and privet hedges.

A cold, cold house. The windows were cloudy with condensation or crazed with ice shivers for months each year. The brown-tiled grate was tiny and the long living-room ate up the smoky coal flames, making draughts that ran in freezing rivers all over the house.

'Were yer born in a barn?' Dad would yell, crouching forward in his armchair, holding out both arms to embrace the puny warmth, swivelling his head and the broad neck purple with raised veins, to accuse any of his four daughters.

Upstairs, all-year winter reigned unchallenged. Never enough blankets, and beds unruly with cast-off coats. Garish linoleum squares bought on HP from the Co-op sat on the stained floorboards and bit into bare feet. The icy water from the lime-crusted tap at the sink made your teeth ache. The bath was used only to catch the drips from washing pegged from string above. Washing of bodies happened on Sunday evenings in big bowls on the kitchen floor, replenished by kettles of boiling water.

Alex paused and stretched, arching her back stiffly, trying to push the past from her shoulders.

Well, perhaps *this* fireplace should go some time, she wondered, scraping the chimney breast with aching arms. Must be 1950s, a late addition to the cottage, and quite out of keeping with the rest. The mottled beige tiles were ugly and the mantelpiece too narrow. Reminded her of Stone-bridge Road.

Tiredness forced her to lay down her tools by late afternoon that first full day. Not the satisfying tiredness of work well done, but the mind-reeling exhaustion of mentally touring the past.

I should walk into the village and be sociable, meet some people, she told herself. See if there's anyone I remember. Which there will be.

But, cross-examining herself, she found she was reluctant and begged for more time. Probably too self-indulgent. Instead of going out, she manhandled the stepladder up the winding stairs on to the landing.

Peter had half boarded the loft when they first moved in. The cardboard boxes and shrouded shapes of unwanted household goods were grey with a layer of fine slate dust from the roof tiles.

Where to begin? A fresh start would be helped by a lighter burden. She felt a strong desire to sift, organize, slim down the clutter of the past. A bit premature? Hardly an urgent task, and one she knew would be painful. Possibly more painful than meeting people in the village. Yet she was too worn out to return to the renovation, too anxious for inactivity. Besides, her deadlines were her own. Still a month till the freight arrived. Before and beyond, the days, weeks, months, stretched ahead like an empty tunnel. And sooner or later there'd be a few walls to meet, looming out of the blackness.

Seeing the row of labelled boxes in the loft made her smile. Archives of such a well-ordered life.

'Hey, d'you make *lists* of your *lists?*' Peter had joked one day.

That would be a day long ago, at the very beginning. That first month at the advertising studio, probably, as Alex was feverishly learning the ropes, memorizing instructions and sizes and times, jotting them all down on scraps of paper taped to the darkroom wall. It was likely she snapped something in reply, curt and defensive. Keep your distance, that was the message. Don't think I don't

14

know I'm young and naïve and likely to be laughed at, working long hours for a pittance in an advertising studio full of men. I'll have you know I chose this, yes, chose it. And it's only a stepping-stone, the place I leap from.

Only, for all her assumed ferocity, the jokes made Alex blush and tremble, even the innocent cartoons and quips they put on the door of the tiny studio darkroom where she photographed artwork to order on a commercial camera that stood taller than she did. 'Some day, my prints will come . . .' That was one of them. Truly, they *were* all so clever, bent over their drawing-boards. And no doubt they saw through the aloofness she thought passed for sophistication.

She failed to disguise, too, the wonder at being allowed to enter such a fascinating new world. She loved it all. Watching over the shoulders of the men at their desks. There was magic to admire – the lightness of touch with an airbrush, the deft positioning of a logo, the brilliance of the half-dozen strokes that assembled a new motif to blazon from a nation's advertising hoardings. Or the skill that sketched a totally original character that within weeks would personify the newest brand of detergent or marmalade. These were the unknown names behind the making of unknown numbers of well-known household names. There was Paul, the studio manager, short-sighted and anxious. Whistling, feet-on-desk Brian, the chief visualizer. Wild and wonderful Steve, head of design. Chain-smoking Maurice, who transformed the roughs into layouts kissed by style and originality. And, of course, Peter, the junior paste-up artist with the straight blond hair, serious square glasses and shabby corduroy trousers.

Sad to think the whole zany, mysteriously rich world had so soon been overtaken by computers. Peter said it often. 'I got out of advertising at the right time, Lexa. All that

15

painstaking work we did by hand – all that's done now in a blip, in a matter of seconds, on a computer screen!'

Blip! A matter of seconds. So many important things were, after all, just a matter of seconds. Like the twitch of a steering-wheel, for instance. Or the jerk that might happen just when a wall was up on the screen, when there was only time for an agonized moan, a moan from deep inside that went on for ever, even when the screen went blank.

Scraping her knuckles, she shifted four boxes nearer to the loft opening. They were too heavy to get down the step-ladder, but she would use plastic bags to ferry the contents in instalments. The weight of history all together might, anyway, crush her otherwise. Safer to sip the cup of suffering.

Crouching to cut through the tape on the lid of one box, she recalled an icebreaker game she had organized once for a women's group meeting in Hong Kong. She asked them to bring in something they would grab if there was a fire, to talk about and show the rest. She expected an assortment of sentimental frippery and photos, a light and frothy opening to the series of studies. But she had forgotten that most of the group were expatriate wives, several of whom arrived empty-handed, embarrassed. Moved at intervals around the world, they regularly transported cut glass and Persian carpets. But they learned to leave what was most valuable and evocative – scrapbooks, old albums, souvenirs – safely stored in a loft or trunk far away. Like she learned to do. Her silly game exposed the women naked of links with all they held most dear, and reminded them of distance and of partings. Some had done their best to play the game, by proxy almost. 'If I had it with me, I would have brought my dear mother's silver locket to show you . . .' But the general air of sobriety convinced her that she had begun badly.

Now here she was, victim to unbidden scenes from her own past, surrounded by her own sweet but somewhat pathetic memorabilia in brown cardboard. Worthless, yet beyond price. Safely sealed.

She backed down the stepladder clutching a batch of bulging manila envelopes and carried them to the kitchen. Making a space on the table, she spread them before her.

She guessed right that these were all from the oldest box. Rifling through these dog-eared bits of paper should be easy, compared to more recent boxes.

Early school reports spilled from the first envelope. They sketched a young Alex she found hard to reconcile with her own recollection of years gone by. What *she* most remembered were the mocking chants and giggles of playground gangs who pressed her hard against the churchyard railings. In these scenes it was always winter. The route to school lay over the exposed common. She had no mittens and, in spite of Mum's woollen headsquare, suffered constant earaches.

The reports told of a success Alex felt she'd missed. The entries neatly inked were almost all 'A's. For Arithmetic (Mechanical), for Arithmetic (Problem), for Reading, Comprehension, Spelling, Composition, History, Geography, Nature Study, Needlework . . . year after yellowed year, nearly always 'A's. And 'A's for Progress and Conduct, though not for Attendance. She wondered if state primary schools of the eighties prepared such detailed reports of today's seven- to eleven-year-olds. Probably not. And the comments! She deciphered scribblings which spoke words of congratulation, or pompous compliments like 'conscientious' and 'reliable' and 'very satisfactory'. Words of commendation that had dazzled Alex the girl.

But, in the end, all was sadly unrealized. Her own

17

version of the story read rather more cruelly. Bringing honour on the junior school across the windswept common from Stonebridge Road by passing an entrance exam for one of the city's top grammar schools brought her bitterness. Even before the first day.

'What's this lot, then?' Dad had demanded.

'Yer never told us about this, my girl. Can't be done. Leastways, not unless we go to see yer Gran on Sunday mornin' . . .'

Here was the offending letter still in the envelope. 'First-form pupils will wear a maroon tunic with flared skirt and square neck, white square-necked blouse with long sleeves, maroon regulation school hat and green hat band, obtainable from the official supplier listed below. Black or brown laced shoes to be worn outdoors (recommended styles: Clarks "Kate" or "Rosamund") and brown sandals to be worn indoors (Clarks "Sunlo" or "Joyance").'

Reaching for the kettle to make a mug of tea, Alex read on, a grudging half-smile on her face, recalling the itchy socks and thick knickers, the science overall, the mud-caked hockey boots.

And she could still picture that Sunday when they took the list of uniform and equipment and walked the six miles to Gran's house on the other, older side of the city.

Dad liked to walk it, he said, but meant that it saved the bus fares. Often Friday night's pay packet was empty by Sunday morning anyway, not least because of Saturday night at the greyhound track. There were always treats on Fridays – fish and chips, pickled onions, Five Boys chocolate bars, sherbert lemons and long stringy toffee pieces known as Everlasting Strips. But the windfall of jollity was mostly spent before the weekend was.

'Pick yer feet up. Walk prop'ly! Yer dawdlin'.'

18

Gran, in black as always since Grandad's slow cancer faded him away, received her son-in-law with pursed-lip suspicion. Sunday calls usually meant money.

'Ma, it's the girl, here. 'Ave a read of this. I never knew she'd 'ave to 'ave all this stuff for that posh school or she wouldna' bin goin'. There's a bit of a grant, 'parently. But it's not much.'

Gran silently stroked the velour of her best table-cover as she sat, put on pink-framed glasses, and studied the letter and its stapled list with shocking prices. Nodding, she eased her bulk up from the table, and pushed through the curtain of plastic strips into the larder that filled the corner of the room. Dad winked at Alex, conspiratorial, but she didn't respond.

On the marble slab at the back of the larder Gran kept a leather handbag with a wad of notes circled by rubber bands. 'Me 'mergency money,' she called it. Alex turned away, agitating the cuttlefish bone clipped against the birdcage bars, so she wouldn't witness the transaction. 'Pretty Joey. Pretty bird,' she cooed. The budgie fluffed its feathers and chirped. It never did talk.

The sombre outfit was duly bought, several sizes too big. 'I'm not paying all this out again tomorrer, my girl. You'll 'ave it with plenty of growin' room or not at all.'

The thicker wad of reports from the grammar school read more realistically. The marks were consistently lower and the comments guarded, faltering. Some faint optimism, with talk of 'making an effort' but more frequently mentions of 'finding difficulties' and 'erratic'. Even, from a Latin teacher, a probing comment about the pupil being 'over-anxious'.

Easy to analyse the downhill slide now, but then it had been all confusion. Alex had struggled not only with academic expectations, but with the puzzling alienation from her peers. She didn't understand the rejection because it took her a surprisingly long time to see that she was different. And then she'd tried to compensate with make-believe and lies.

She remembered Adele, with her single glossy dark plait and aristocratic nose. She was one of the girls who pushed her hardest.

'Mummy says we're all going to Spain for half-term, Alexandra. Of course, it means I won't get to ride Monarch all week, but I'll make it up to him. I'm *so* looking forward to the beach. I've got a new red bikini. And Daddy says in my heels and long dress I could easily pass for eighteen and get into the casino. What about you?'

The last was a challenge, the eyebrows arched in faint amusement.

Did they believe the fables she offered them, mumbling, hesitatingly at first and then with increasing boldness? Probably not. What an education! It had taught her the art of deception. The science of self-defence.

Enough for today! She was getting cynical. She assembled the reports in date order and slipped them back into the envelope.

Strangely enough, she felt a genuine affection for the huge girls' school, a warmth which lingered long after she left, out of keeping with what it had given her. Misplaced nostalgia. These days she was able to be more objective about the effect on the young Alex of straddling the social divide. Living in two worlds, one harshly real, one invented as she daydreamed on the bus to school or loitered in the cloakroom after lessons, was not without its penalty. And not without its burden. Alex had paid a heavy price, coined in guilt and anxiety.

TWO

The next morning Alex slept late, the night disturbed by the old nightmare of the impenetrable grey wall. She woke surprised at the brilliance of an unexpected blue sky reflecting into every corner of the bedroom. She'd forgotten to close the curtains and lay watching the dancing dust-motes above the edge of the sleeping-bag, and, beyond and unfocused, the fragile leaves stirring on a tree preparing to be stripped for winter.

The blueness of the sky was washed, without the depth of Asian skies, but still it cheered her. She thought with longing of the bright sealing-wax palms and the bank of luxuriant bougainvillaea with its purple-pink papery blooms that had framed the morning view from the balcony of the staff flat in Singapore. Sometimes, when the heat drove them from sleep, Alex and Peter would sit in silence on the rattan sofa with its perpetually damp cushions, and watch the sky wake, passing from blue-blackness to vivid blueness with a speed that amazed. The chitchats that scolded and scuttled all night disappeared and the day became the domain of the cheeky black and white mynahs.

Reaching for her dressing-gown, Alex thanked God for a new day, knowing that her thankfulness was as changeable as the weather and feeling chastened to recognize it.

Sitting over coffee and toast in the kitchen, she froze when she heard a hesitant knocking at the front door. She felt caught off guard.

'Alex, it *is* you! Someone said they'd seen you drive through the village. Why didn't you come over and let me know you were back? How are you? Are you staying long? Have you got all you need?'

'Helen, come in. Have some coffee. Sorry, I'm not properly dressed.'

Somehow, it was easier than she feared. Naturally, after a few opening pleasantries, Helen edged towards mentioning the accident, like a blind woman feeling with her toes for the edge of the pavement. But she was easily deflected, sent on a detour, sensitive enough to know that Alex wasn't ready to talk. And Alex was grateful. Her pulse slowed.

'Still teaching at the village school?'

Helen shook her cool blonde bob energetically.

'Yes, for my sins! I'd like to get a post in Oxford but it's not easy to find the right opening. Numbers are still falling here. We might have to close a class next year.'

'Helen, I haven't got a washing-machine that works here, until I can get around to seeing if the old one's worth repairing. I was wondering . . .'

'Gosh yes! Any time. Bring your washing round. Just like old times when you and Peter moved . . .'

Her enthusiasm checked only for a split second.

'I'll give you a spare key and you can come over whenever you like. It's only me here most of the time.

Sarah's in her second year at Nottingham now, you know. Just gone back.'

Alex relaxed a little more. It was going to be all right. People would really understand.

Helen rose.

'Here,' she said, awkwardly fumbling in her shopping basket.

'The latest church magazine. Probably all the times of the services and everything are just as you remember them. Things don't change much, not in a place like this.'

She started to laugh, but, suddenly seeing the doubt in Alex's eyes, stopped herself.

'Yes, well, when you're ready, Alex dear.'

She dropped the little yellow magazine on to the table.

'It's *so* nice to have you back.'

She sniffed and made a clumsy attempt at an embrace, but Alex was wooden and suddenly there were tears in her eyes.

'I'll see myself out. Bye for now.'

The breeze caught the door and slammed it as Helen left. For a moment, the cottage felt unbearably empty. With an effort, Alex wiped her eyes on her sleeve. I'm *not* alone, she whispered to herself. Jehovah Shammah! The Lord who is there. Solitude she could cope with, even welcome. But aloneness would be not possible.

By noon the following day, the walls of the sitting-room were bare of paper. Sweeping the soggy heaps into a plastic sack, she tentatively lifted a corner of the old carpet with the scraper. It came up easily, leaving a residue of grey dust as the old foam backing disintegrated. Might as well get this up now as later. There was little furniture in the room – just the old sofa, a gateleg table and a couple of chairs. She shifted everything into the hallway.

When the floorboards were exposed and washed, the room looked and felt very different. Thankfully, Alex lost herself in the rhythm of the work. She mixed several batches of filler in an old saucer and worked systematically, covering cracks in the walls and smoothing over the gaps where skirtings shrank away. Once or twice, she wished for music or a radio. But generally, the quietness was like a reward and she rested in its wholesomeness. She worked hard, pressed and pushed herself, but, for all the growing autumnal goldenness outside, it was still not a good day.

'Lord, you know I need a new day,' she whispered over and over into the night.

Waking again, but unrefreshed and disoriented, she couldn't remember the date and frantically thrashed about on her back in the confusion of sleeping-bag and blanket, trying desperately to work it out. Be calm! She'd left Hong Kong on the 22nd. That meant Heathrow and arriving at the cottage on the 23rd. Then there was the first day, the day she'd opened the loft. Then the next morning when Helen had come. That would be the 25th, the day before yesterday. So today had to be the 27th.

Oh, God, I've missed it! How could I!

Dates were so important, more so now than ever.

She decided to walk into the village. It would be a penance for forgetfulness. But also a time to compose her tumbling memories.

Her anorak felt too thin, but she found a woollen scarf and old leather gloves in a box in the bike shed and felt pleased to discover she didn't at all mind what she looked like. It must be a sign of maturity, she thought, to be released from the dictates of fashion. Or was it that she had no-one to impress any more?

Scuffling through the few fallen leaves around the gate,

24

Alex felt momentarily as exhilarated as a child in the chill air and wished she was wearing wellington boots. The world was russet and rosy, cold but with not a hint yet of dampness. For five years she'd not seen or felt a British autumn. Her one brief return had straddled spring and summer. Did children still gather conkers and stick leaves on coloured paper for classroom walls? Innocent pleasures.

It had been an autumn day when she'd become a poet and resolved to write for the rest of her life. She must have been twelve or thirteen, wearing that same bulky dark uniform financed with Gran's 'mergency money. She was skipping through leaves on the path up to the school sports field, carrying a hockey stick. Somehow she was partnered that day with a girl who was in awe of her. For one inspirational moment the beauty of falling and fallen leaves overtook her and pushed her into rhyme. She danced over self-consciousness, opened her mouth and words tumbled out.

'Alexandra, did you write that? It was lovely. Did you do it for Composition? All that about the bare trees and the yellow leaves and the wind and . . . and everything.'

'It just came. Out of my head. It's all in there. I'm going to write it all down.'

The girl's eyes shone and Alex was warmed by a sensation of admiration that took her breath away. She laughed and ran ahead, not caring about the stiff tunic folds that chafed her legs to soreness.

A delivery van swished by in the narrow lane leading to the village, and Alex shrugged deeper into the woollen scarf. Bravery demanded she would go to the village minimart and buy some milk, some fresh bread.

But how had she forgotten the date? For the first time in thirteen years? Unlucky for some.

'I'll always remember the day I first met you. That pale green raincoat, very short. Too short! Gorgeous legs.' That was his promise.

And now the first time to remember it alone, Alex had forgotten. She accused herself. How could she? A September Monday. Her first nine o'clock start in the big wide world. There he was, crouched over his drawing board, blond hair like a shaft of sunlight. Wearing an open-necked black shirt and those awful ink-stained corduroy trousers. And when the studio manager said, 'Peter knows how to operate the darkroom. He'll show you how it all works,' she thought, 'I hope he doesn't think I'm going to fall for him, just because he's teaching me my job. I'm not going to be that typical, writing myself into a woman's magazine.'

It had been a kind of premonition, or an awareness of some deep magic already at work. Because, beginning on that day, fresh from school, full of big ideas, yet hurting from a long summer when she stood on the brink of nothingness and pulled back, she began, inexorably, to love Peter. And that September day they marked ever after, making a catalogue of memories. Till this year.

Alex found a stile where she could sit and rest like an invalid from her runaway thoughts. The panorama of green and brown falling away downhill from the roadside soothed her. But the years kept falling away, too.

Until Peter there had been no memorable dates in the calendar. Nothing worth remembering. Not even birthdays. Certainly not boyfriends.

'Sweet sixteen and never been kissed.' Wasn't that how the song went?

'So what *do* you do on the *Herald*, Dave? Are you a reporter?' Alex had insisted.

26

The social club was blurred with people and her cheeks burned. She shuffled her feet in the birthday brown shoes that were already pinching. She had to yell over the blare of the jukebox. *'Walking back to happiness,'* roared out Helen Shapiro.

'What do you want to drink, birthday girl?' Dave asked, grabbing her hand with his own, hot and moist.

She thought, desperately. Reviewing some of those cloakroom conversations. Gin and tonic? Martini? Rum and Coke? Cider?

'Shandy,' she blurted out. 'Just a small one.'

They pushed through the talking bodies and blue smoke clouds, past the snooker table to the bar.

'Oom-pah-oh-yeah-yeah,' sang out the deep voice.

'So, is that what you are? A reporter? I'm going to work on a newspaper one day,' Alex persisted. Birthdays make you bold.

'Not exactly a reporter,' he grinned, pushing back dark curly hair with one hand and raising his glass with the other. 'More on the marketing and circulation side, you might say.'

She was impressed. Marketing and circulation.

It was six weeks before she found out he meant driving a newspaper delivery van. And, angry and foolish but quite clear of her motives, she said goodbye. His lips, hot and moist like his hands, meant nothing to her.

Alex shivered and slid down from the stile. She walked more purposefully now, and the minimart was soon in sight on one corner of the triangular green.

The shop had one of those bells that caught and clanged when the door opened. Inside it was deserted, but Alex heard a shuffling from behind a curtain next to the counter and a cheerful, muffled voice called out, 'Be with you in a minute, dearie. Just getting some stock unpacked.'

Alex began filling a wire basket. Muesli, milk, bread rolls, tinned soup, pâté. A blast of chill air preceded by a split second the renewed ringing of the bell.

'Hi! It's Alex, isn't it! Remember me?'

'Mandy, right?'

The younger woman smiled, shedding sheepskin mitts, stuffing them into her dufflecoat pocket. She shook her fluffy, pale ginger curls. Her freckled face was rosy from the wind.

'Really turned cold today, hasn't it? Shouldn't be surprised if there was an early frost tonight. I bet you really feel it, don't you? I mean, coming from the tropics and that. You back for long this time?'

Alex nodded, her eyes absent, wandering lost over the shelves. She ransacked her memory.

'How's Shaun? And . . . and the baby?'

'Shaun's fine. Still working at his dad's garage. The money's not great but we get by. Stephen's at playgroup now. And Darren's a year old next month. I still go to the mums and toddlers coffee morning at St Matthew's. Remember the first time I came, that summer you were here and you showed those slides of the children's home in Hong Kong?'

Alex smiled.

'Darren's fast asleep in the buggy outside, if you want to take a look at him. He looks like an angel when he's sleeping, but he can be a bit of a monkey when he's awake!'

'And,' with a bashful grin, patting her stomach through the grey duffle, 'there's another on the way. Only just. Actually, you're the first to know. Can't keep it to myself! The doctor confirmed it this morning. Not due till next May. We're hoping for a little girl this time.'

Walking away from the green, swinging her plastic bag, Alex felt a familiar icy stiffness in her chest. Over the years she had steeled herself to this kind of conversation, this kind of encounter with the glowing glory of motherhood, and she had confidence in her ability to cope. She took some deep breaths. Naturally, at a time like this . . . She counted off the months. In fact, it was only an almost pregnancy-length since the world had fallen apart, so, of course, it was bound to hit home a little harder. She excused herself for her too-ready tears.

Yet, another old movie began rolling relentlessly in her head.

'Unless we run more exhaustive tests, Mrs Davis, we can't really be sure what's causing the problem. Now, if you'll let me pass you on to a colleague at the clinic, I'm sure he'll come up with a helpful diagnosis. One of the best men in Singapore. There's a great deal that can be done these days.'

'Thank you, doctor. As I said, I'll think about it a bit more, talk it over with my husband. But I think not.'

He didn't understand. His white-coated efficiency made it all sound so logical. But creating life wasn't just a biological process. She tried to tell him that God came into it. More. God didn't *just* come into it, God *was* it.

The things people said. The way people looked. The way they assumed. 'I expect we'll be hearing the patter of tiny feet some day soon.' Or some such cliché. Or worse, some smirking aside with lowered lids, some smutty challenge to manhood, some urging to fit the mould.

She rehearsed it all with Peter again that afternoon after the consultation. Not only for her own sake but so that she knew just what to say when she was constantly challenged on every hand, by friends, by the family. Believing, yet she needed help with the unbelief. Meanwhile, sitting on the kitchen counter was a card from Anne to say they had a second son. And Mary already had three little ones.

'I shouldn't even have bothered to go. The doctors just don't understand. When I'm here with you, talking, just the two of us, it makes sense. It sounds sane and reasonable and right. Perfectly right. If our lives are God's and we claim he's in control, we *can't* go running off to technology for help when there's something we don't like.'

Running her hand distractedly through her hair, restlessly pacing the apartment, she spelled it all out, like they'd both done so many times before.

'Childlessness isn't a disease or . . . or a tumour that can be operated on. Life's a gift from God, so he can choose not to give it. But, in that doctor's room this afternoon, like in so many other places and times, it sounds quite ludicrous, quite weak somehow, even though I know it's strong really. The really weak thing would be to let them all have their way. Not stand firm by our principles.'

Now rounding on him, her voice a little high, wavering.

'When I'm with you, I believe it all. But these so-called experts sound so self-assured, so, *so reasonable*. And Peter, even if there is some simple medical or physical problem that could be put right, we believe, don't we, that God could intervene and do it if . . . if he wanted us to have a child? Just tell me again, tell me we're right!'

Now in his arms, trembling.

'Shh, relax. Be still. Don't upset yourself like this again. God *is* in control. We've chosen, we're going to trust him and he won't let us down.'

He sighed, sad, hurting and helpless, nothing new to say.

'We've been over all this before, my own love. The

30

principles would be enough in themselves. But there's more. We need to be straightforwardly practical, even though it's painful. How could we possibly justify the expense of fertility explorations and treatments? I wouldn't feel right about claiming for it when we know how tight SaveAid's budget is this year. Putting it crudely, money for us to try for a baby – which might not work – means less for the leprosy clinic in Calcutta or the women's hostel in Bangkok. How could we do it?' He crushed her in his arms, wanting to smother the pain with the ferocity of present love.

Later, cradling her in the silence of renewed resignation, he kissed away her tears. The ceiling fan whirred, rippling the cotton sheet on the bed as the purple shadows deepened and another dusk fell like a curtain.

'I want a baby every bit as much as you do. You know that, don't you? At the same time, if we had one, well, SaveAid would lose a valuable worker. One of the best. And, being very selfish, I'd lose a wonderful travelling companion. What would I do without you to keep me sane? All those desperate hotel rooms would be awful on my own. There are compensations, aren't there? Come on, darling. No cooking tonight. Let's shower and go to Sami's for a curry.'

Alex reached the cottage, running the last few yards as to a refuge.

Pointless not to admit that there were times when the injustice of it all threatened to overturn the constantly affirmed decision. But in all her saner, surer moments she felt they were right to accept the barren womb as no less a token of God's sovereignty than all his good gifts. Only now the emptiness was so final. No room for manoeuvre. No room for miracle. No comfort in her arms.

Or was it final? Her runaway mind conjured up a little lost face, brown eyes questioning, puzzled red mouth pursed in an 'oh' of confusion. But an effort of will made the image vanish.

Alex put away the groceries and bargained with herself over the manufactured priorities that pressed in on her. She would devote the rest of the day to the cottage. First, a coat of white emulsion on the sitting-room ceiling, and undercoat on the skirtings and doors. She needed urgently to make progress and see results, fearful of losing momentum on a project that carried all the import of a last will and testament.

But before she began work, she would make a phone call, to prepare the way. For the visit tomorrow.

THREE

There was a crunch of loose gravel as she curved the Metro to a halt below the stone entrance steps to Cairnhill Grange.

'Oh, how lovely! He hardly ever gets any visitors.'

The nurse was very young and couldn't know that such simple words were cold knives to a hurting heart.

Alex followed her through an archway, along a tiled hall to the day-room. She eyed the pale pink walls and extravagantly flowered curtains and wondered how such a colour scheme could feel antiseptic.

The day-room was just as she remembered it from a brief visit prompted by a short-lived crisis over two years previously. She'd rushed home while the country was red, white and blue with patriotism, fighting the Falklands War. Dad won his own little battle, too. And she was able to leave by the time everyone was cooing over the newborn Prince William.

The room was narrow, with one long wall glazed and letting in the view of a sloping lawn, now nodding with a border of pale yellow chrysanthemums. A dozen elderly men and women were slumped in high-backed plastic upholstered chairs, propped like puppets with wedges of pillows.

'Hello, Dad. It's me. Alex.'

She dragged over a footstool and perched on it, reaching out to cover with her own the old man's blue-veined hand as it rested trembling like a sparrow on the nest of beige cellular blanket. Hard to believe he was still in his fifties.

'Thought you'd be coming one of these days. Took yer time, though, didn't yer?'

The voice was guttural and slow. The fleshy head turned with effort, watery eyes stared from under heavy lids. There was a tremor in the gaze. The once powerful neck had wasted and the skin stretched whitely over the prominent Adam's apple.

'How are you, Dad? I spoke to Sister Hendry on the phone yesterday. She said you were doing pretty well, considering.'

'Ah well, she don't know much. I shouldn't take too much notice of these medical types if I was you, love. Most of the doctors that comes round, they'm straight from school. Still wet behind the ears.'

There was a silence, broken only by the scraping of trolley wheels in a distant corridor and the rasping cough of another patient.

He shifted in the chair and seemed to gather energy.

'I don't think they knows what's really up with yer Dad's stomach. I keeps telling 'em, I says, "Doc, this stomach's givin' me bloody gyp. All night. Can't sleep." They just gives I a few more pills. Stand me up, my girl, and I'll rattle, I swear I'll rattle.'

The face twisted into a wry grin, became more animated and alive.

'Tea with two sugars, isn't it, Mr Travers? And would your visitor like some?'

'Yeah, she'll stay for a cuppa. Won't yer? This is me eldest, sister. Alexandra. We give all our girls royal names. Little princesses. Two of 'em lives abroad. Alex is one of 'em. Leastways, she did. And Annie, too. In Australia. But I'm thinking she'll be back, too, before long. Once the divorce is settled. Then I'll get to see those two grandsons of mine.'

The cups clattered down on to a side table.

Dad eyed the sister's retreating back. He winked at Alex.

'She's a bit of all right, that one. Even though she's a darkie. Knows how to have a laugh now and again. Some of 'em in here, they got faces like pokers. Proper tartars. Can't take a joke.'

There were a few faltering exchanges about daughters, grandchildren, brothers, uncles.

Suddenly, his face clouded.

'This you've bin through, it's a bad business, Alex. A bad business. Got yer letter. Young Lizzie and Terry came, read it out to me, two, three times. Couldn't take it in, first off. How're yer gonna cope, love? Are you badly off? Still mixed up with all this church lark? If so, then I hope yer getting what's due. I'd help you out if I could, I 'ope you knows that. Always thought I'd 'ave a bit put by in me last years, but it didn't work out that way. I'm right glad yer mother's not alive. This 'ud finish 'er, this 'ud. Don't bear thinkin' about much, do it? It's a rum life, that's fer sure.'

Then he lapsed into silence and Alex knew she need not reply, nor could she. They sat, companionably enough, lost

35

in thought, staring out at the bowing chrysanthemum heads, heavy and wilting on the stalks.

Alex was remembering the last time she'd seen her mother.

'Alex, Alex!' Dad was shouting up the stairs.

'Come 'ere a minute. Get yer coat on quick. Yer mother's gone walkin' again. Go and fetch 'er back, there's a good girl. She's only bin gone a minute or two.'

A common climax to the shouts from downstairs. The four girls had retreated upstairs, guilty, under a fusillade of threats and slamming of doors.

'You bloody stupid woman! I'm telling you I ain't goin' in to that fact'ry no more and it's no use you goin' on and on about it. I've 'ad as much as I can stick from that foreman and I ain't takin' another day of it. I've asked fer me cards. So, just shut up, will yer? I'll go an' sign on tomorrer. Get somethin' better.'

This time the sounds were the same; the outcome different.

Buttoning her coat, Alex ran towards the common. Mum always took the same route. She'd be grey-faced, headscarf on, head down, braced into the wind, hands in pockets, walking stubbornly into nowhere. And Alex would catch her up and, panting, link through her arm and walk, too.

'He doesn't really mean it, Mum. He says to come home. It'll be all right.'

'I can only take so much. I'm sick and tired. Another decent job down the drain. Another struggle till he can get the next. And how long will *that* one last?'

There was no more anger left. Only a bone weariness.

'Us kids . . . Come back. I bet he's sorry. He won't say, I know, but . . .' The words weak and, anyway, the bent figure inconsolable.

She began crying softly into the relentless cold wind. There were a few stars overhead, stabbing the blackness. But she didn't look up. Nor back. And took no notice of the child on her arm. Not this time.

Now Alex stood up, tearing her eyes from the ragged patches of yellow flowers.

'I'd better be going now, Dad. It's a long drive back to the cottage and I'd rather make it before dark.'

He nodded, stared vacantly, pouted purplish lips.

'Anything I can bring you? Next time?'

'An' when'll that be then? Next time?'

The voice was petulant, as of an overlooked child.

'Soon. I won't leave it too long next time. Promise.'

Hard for Alex not to feel suffocated in a mountain of weeping resentment. Here was a man who'd squeezed what he could out of life, like a dog worrying at a bone. He'd taken by force things he'd never earned or had a right to, but was left empty-handed. A man for whom giving was an alien experience. But he was still alive. Defiantly alive. Whereas . . .

'The Lord gives, and the Lord takes away. Blessed be the name of the Lord,' she whispered again and again as she drove into the dusk. And she prayed for motherless children, near and far.

Time at the cottage passed industriously enough. By the end of the week Alex was taking comfort in renewed walls. Still bare, but now edged with gleaming white at the skirting below and bold jade at the picture rail above. This room was becoming a little oasis of brightness, and for now Alex couldn't consider how much there was still to tackle in the rest of the cottage.

Today she was ready to begin pasting the Anaglypta paper to the walls. It was an unusual heritage, but wallpapering was the solitary skill Alex had received from her father. Home decorating was quite a hobby with him, and, since he was a heavy smoker, stripping walls and making way for fresh paper was a regular occurrence at Stonebridge Road. Strangely proud, Alex stood in for a son on these occasions, passing razor knife and brush and folded cloth alternately, wiping the excess paste from the dining table between each cut and raised length, watching as he matched flower stem to leaf and gilded frond to gaudy berry.

He wouldn't have approved of their choice for this room at the cottage – a simple embossed paper to be painted over with plain cream.

'You want sommat with a bit of life in it,' he'd say, standing back to admire a wall of violent fruit and rampant colour.

There was just one time she'd asked him to do some wallpapering for her. It was a kind of peace treaty.

After that eventful summer when the whole world turned upside down, Alex felt like a lodger at home through her first few months at the advertising studio. In the springtime, when she started working on the newspaper, she left home on the strength of fulfilled ambition. It was a miserable parting, the climax to weeks of raised voices.

Julia, one of the girls from the church, was moving into a flat by the railway station and offered to share. It was on the second floor of a thin terraced house in The Baulk. Just two rooms, joined by a minute passageway in which there was a sink, water heater and tiny Belling hotplate.

The living-room was generously proportioned, with a broad chimney breast, and two windows overlooking the grim derelict bonded warehouses beyond.

'I'll get Dad to help us do it up,' Alex ventured, daring, to Julia the day they moved in. 'It'll be a kind of olive branch.'

And so it proved. Dad was flattered, ready to put the past summer away.

'You just let me know soon as you've got the paper and paint bought. I'll be down there like a shot and 'ave it done in no time.'

Tastes change. At the opening of the seventies, big and bold was in. They bought paper with heavy geometric designs in dramatic dark blues and purples for the fireplace wall, and woodchipped the other three, painting them bright orange. She supposed it was fitting. Such brightness was in keeping with her vision of herself as the new trainee reporter.

Peter put up pine shelves in the alcove next to the fireplace at The Baulk. By that time they did everything together and talked of engagement, the next summer, on his twenty-first birthday. The early verbal sparring was over, Peter had made a spiritual commitment that matched her own, and anxiety had given way to an intoxicating, reckless absorption in each other.

These days she was out of practice. By dusk at the cottage Alex was wearily trimming the last piece of paper around the first doorway. Only half way. She would carry on tomorrow. Living overseas in rented accommodation with no DIY to do had made her soft. That's what Dad would say.

That evening she retrieved a shoebox of old photos from the loft. She had a faint memory of some photos taken at The Baulk and wanted to find them.

Disappointingly, they were black and white, tiny prints. In one, Alex sat on the low wall at the back of the house, thin legs crossed at the ankles, long dark hair tied back, squinting into the sunshine. She wore a white top, short-sleeved, knitted by her Gran, and a forgotten skirt that was very short. She looked fragile.

In another, she was standing with Peter and the Honda motorbike on the road outside The Baulk. Peter was cradling his crash helmet. She studied the familiar slow, shy smile, the blond fringe almost obscuring his eyes. She scanned the print carefully for something she might have missed, but found nothing. The next one was of Julia grinning idiotically, standing by the front door, the same Julia who was to look so demure in bridesmaid blue. She was carrying a cardboard box. Could it have been taken on moving-in day?

The time at The Baulk had been a short but important interlude of three years. No longer a schoolgirl, Alex had outgrown Stonebridge Road but was a beginner at independence. Julia, a couple of years older, carried her uncomplainingly during the flat-sharing. She made sure the rent was paid on time, borrowed bedding from her mother for Alex, showed her how to use a launderette.

As Alex reached again into the box of photos, the phone rang.

'Hi. Alex? It's me. Mandy.'

Her voice was breathless, rushed. A toddler was whimpering in the background.

'I feel really bad. Someone was talking about you outside the school gate. And that was the first I heard about it, honest. About your husband. I'm sorry. You must have thought me a bit thoughtless, you know, when I bumped into you earlier. I didn't say I was sorry or anything. But I didn't know.'

Alex flailed around for one or two comforting sentiments, wondering at her own need to set Mandy at ease. And closed off the conversation as soon as she could.

She put the photos aside. A clutch of handwritten poems shared the same box. The most prolific period for the girl poet. Certainly, the output trailed to virtually nothing within a couple of years. But poetry had seemed to be a vital ingredient of distilling distress in those earlier days.

She remembered the first line of one, but couldn't find it. 'Over the cold chimneys another day breaks. Solitary in her penance, the girl wakes.' All the poems had been that dreadful. That one was about the awakening that took place.

The awakening. The year 1971 had started with her eighteenth birthday and the closing two terms of her school career. She was doing badly and knew it. Concentration was hard. Wasn't life supposed to be wonderful? Years of trying to keep up with everything left her baffled.

It was like running a race with a secret handicap. The essays, the projects, the swotting for exams – well, she had no more of that than anyone else. But when she went up into the bedroom and balanced her books on her knees, she was acutely aware of penalties she felt she didn't deserve. Like the bitter creeping cold, the gnawing hunger pains, the writing by moonlight when there was no shilling for the electricity meter. She felt the injustice keenly but was no campaigner. Instead of revising history notes, she hugged her knees and composed romantic poems in green biro.

Trouble was, some burdens were complicated, and these she could lay at no-one's doorstep but her own. She had a growing recognition of the self-inflicted problems that kept her running and panting to stand still. Like the

41

cheating and lying, which started as excusable self-defence but ballooned with fantasy into a whole alternative personality Alex neither liked nor knew. The web of deceit, self-woven, was choking her. Her memory began to let her down. Things she invented – holidays in Brighton, a collection of Beatles records, even a boy called Mark who'd taken her to see *The Sound of Music* and held her hand in the dark – began to escape dangerously from her mind and she made stupid contradictions in cloakroom chat sessions.

And then there was the shoplifting.

In the beginning she'd justified it quite easily. It's wrong that I'm hungry; therefore I will take what I need. Chocolate bars or bags of pink and white marshmallows were smuggled out of the Spar supermarket in her schoolbag. She wasn't good at thieving and the violent heartbeating exhausted her. But somehow she never got caught. Sometimes she felt it would help if a heavy hand of accusation descended on her shoulder. From food she felt compelled to move on to other things. Nail polish, lipsticks, stockings. Just to close the gap, she argued with herself. Once she wanted to give a teacher a Christmas gift and took a wooden ornament, a six-inch Viking doll with shield and fluffy hair, courtesy of Debenhams.

When spring came, mounting inner tension and shame were ripe, bursting towards the summer showdown.

In a fit of something akin to disillusionment and self-disgust, Alex threw in the couple of places she was holding for second-rate universities. Teachers took this as a personal insult and retreated icily. Well, they'd never regarded aspirations to journalism as particularly honourable, anyway. Most of the girls they turned out from the grammar school went into medicine, law or teaching. Those who didn't quite make the grade were steered into secretarial college or nursing. But journalism? They washed their hands of her.

She felt the rejection keenly, but refused to show it. It sharpened her determination. She spent hours in the reference library, systematically writing letters of application to all the editors in the five counties nearest home. But it seemed no-one wanted a trainee reporter. The way she described it to Dad was, 'I could paper a room with rejection letters.'

Strangely, it brought them briefly closer together. 'Never mind, love.' He understood thwarted ambition. A domineering father had pushed him into the Army to free up a bed space at Northwood Grove. He was glad she wasn't going to university because his conviction was that she should be out earning. He tolerated her talk of newspapers and offered the advice that 'a nice office job would be a safe ticket for life'. She talked to no-one else about her frustrated ambitions, a tortoise withdrawing its head into a shell of cynicism, hiding the scars of disappointment.

Meantime, school was out and she felt the future fall like a wedge between her and the rest of the leavers. While they talked courses and tutors and halls of residence, she rode the bus downtown and got herself a job for the summer, at a brand new hamburger café.

Surprisingly, she enjoyed waitressing at Chico's. She tacked up the hem on the black nylon overall, pulled the white lacy apron tight at the waist, and hoped it made her look pale and interesting. The pay was awful but she was quick and efficient and the tips were good. She felt at home at Chico's, especially in the evenings when the orange lights dimmed to give the café the romantic atmosphere of a warm cave. She promised herself she wouldn't shoplift any more, and kept her promise – more or less.

Chico's specialized in daily disasters, and Alex grew accustomed to putting things straight. The evening cook was a harassed middle-aged woman with problems. She often reported in late or drunk or both. Alex covered for Dora, slapping burgers and fried eggs on the sizzling griddle, popping sesame bun halves into the toaster, whipping up lavish chocolate sundaes in cocktail glasses. The kitchen regularly ran out of paper serviettes or tomato pickle. Throwing an anorak over her uniform, Alex dashed out of the back door to the supermarket. 'What would we do without you?' Dora or one of the others said, actually meaning it, and Alex worked even harder.

From time to time, the manager himself would flash her an appreciative smile.

'I come from Persia,' he told her, and the soft slow way he pronounced it was like the purring of a cat, so that she thought of him as a pampered, exotic breed of feline. He was slight, hardly taller than Alex, with a smooth, olive baby face. At thirty-two his fine black hair was already thinning. He held himself remote from the staff, appearing each day in a dark suit and white shirt. He glanced at Alex from under long black lashes as he perched on a stool to count money at the till or hovered in the storeroom checking invoices.

'You look especially sad tonight,' he suggested one evening.

She blushed.

'It's nothing. Not really. Just another letter today, from a weekly in Bridgwater, another newspaper that doesn't need me. I was hoping they would ask me for an interview.'

'Ah, the girl who wants to be a reporter. Yes?' He stared at her with his intense brown eyes.

She continued to slice the sesame buns, heaping them on to a metal tray.

'You know, I have my sadness, too. My disappointments. Sometimes people can help each other when they are sad, don't you think? Maybe if we tell each other our sadness, we can be happy?'

She held her breath. Her hands were shaking.

'Look, sad girls must take break from work now and then. You finish early tonight, OK? Boss's orders. Then you and me, we go for nice meal together. Forget our sadness. Eight o'clock. Is a deal?'

FOUR

Sweet and sour pork balls swam lurid pink on the rice. Alex sat with Sed in his van near the river. They balanced polystyrene boxes on their laps, spearing mouthfuls with plastic forks.

'Really? First time you eat Chinese?'

'Honest! I love it. It's great!'

Sed was keen to win her sympathy. Neither at the time nor later could she decide how much of what he told her was true. He spoke of a young wife, fair and lovely but treacherous, who had left him two months earlier for someone he always referred to with venom as 'that white Jew boy'. He also had a father dying of cancer in Tehran who sent him weekly letters pleading for him to return. He was saving for the airfare home, but managing Chico's didn't pay well and it was going to take at least six months.

He said he'd been watching Alex for weeks and thought she was beautiful.

Compliments were a new experience and made her dizzy.

'I really wonder,' he added, reaching over the handbrake to stroke her knee lightly, 'I wonder if I might not be falling in love with you.'

Alex knew she was acting a part but lacked the experience to do otherwise. She nodded thoughtfully, seriously, at appropriate times during his confidences, her attention wandering as she tried to manage the takeaway without spilling it. The nylon uniform kept riding up her thighs and the zip pressed cold into her back. She began to feel sick and asked Sed to drive her home. She had to be in before 10.30 or Dad would be mad, really mad, she assured him. Mercifully, he consented without protest. He dropped her off at the common, pulling her to him for a brief kiss. His olive skin and breath were strangely aromatic.

She ran through the dusk, the cooling breeze like a slap on her hot cheeks.

She crept upstairs into the boxroom. As eldest, she had the tiny room to herself; her three sisters shared the larger front bedroom. She entered soundlessly, not putting on the light. Dropping her handbag on the bed, she closed the door and then opened the corner cupboard. Fumbling inside, she found the box of matches and struck one. She lit the candle end, and dripped wax into the saucer till she could glue it upright.

The cupboard was her only privacy. Really no more than a clothes-hanging space, but she made it serve more urgent purposes.

A bronze bar ran at shoulder height across the width of the cupboard, the bracket supporting a wooden shelf of her stories and poems. Pulling the door closed, she knelt by the upturned cardboard box on the bare floorboards. The box was covered by one of Mum's headsquares, Paisley patterned, and on that rested the first four books she owned and loved.

The first was a faded blue hardback copy of *Five Go Off In A Caravan*, inscribed from her Gran on her sixth birthday. The second was *Black Beauty*, a Christmas gift one year from Mum.

The third was a small green book called *Let God Be True*, beautifully illustrated with a frontispiece of a golden-haired girl and a handsome youth standing below a tree luxuriant with fruit. At their feet lay a snowy lamb and a slumbering lion. One day, years before, she had been at Gran's house when two women had called at the door and talked animatedly and at length. Gran had finally returned into the living-room from the long hallway carrying a sheaf of magazines and the green book.

'Had to buy these before they'd go away and leave me in peace,' she grumbled. 'They said they'd call again to talk to me next week. Not if I have my way. I'll make sure I'm out the house next Tuesday. Think I'll go down the bingo. Mavis said they put the jackpot up.'

'Can I have the book, Gran? It's got gold letters.'

'Of course, love. You take it. I don't read much these days. *Woman's Realm*, that's my favourite. I have it on order from Elsie at the corner shop.'

So *Let God Be True* had joined the others and been cherished in the cupboard shrine. For some reason, she had never read it, and years later when she understood it was a Jehovah's Witness publication, she tore it apart, shocked.

But she had thought of it then as a kind of holy book, and placed it reverently next to the fourth book on the cardboard altar: a very small black Bible with tiny print. This was also a gift, from Dad, for her twelfth birthday.

'Look, love, if it's what you really wants, well . . . you can 'ave it, of course. I thought you was set on 'aving roller skates, you said. But it's your birthday, you choose. It's not that high-falutin school putting funny ideas into yer 'ead, is it? Because if so, I'll be up there, sortin' em out. You take my word for it, my girl, all this church lark's a bit of a racket. What do you think they does with all that collection money every week? Line their own pockets, that's what. Church is not for the likes of us, you take my word for it. All poker faces, the lot of 'em.'

The junior-school anniversary service had been her only entrance to the church nearest to Stonebridge Road, and all that happened there, though sweetly ceremonial, remained an unreality. Only once had she revisited St John's, when she was fourteen or fifteen. The congregation was small and elderly and the singing insipid. As she stood to file out of the pew at the end of the service, she was conscious of hooded and hostile eyes. She slid out of the side door and never returned.

But still Alex treasured the black Bible and over the years longed for it to reveal the mystical or magical qualities she was sure it possessed. She started to read it many times, and knew well the majestic opening chapters on the creation, and Adam and Eve. Cain's violence chilled her. Noah's rainbow enchanted her. Beyond that it got more difficult. There was the burning of sheep and the strangling of turtledoves, blood and idols, tribal genealogies and cities of refuge. Though fascinating, this was an altogether remote world, a secret walled garden glimpsed in a soft-focus dream but not entered. Dissatisfied, she read no more for a while, but kept it reverently on the altar and pressed summer flower petals between the pages till they were blotched with brown. It was a superstitious attachment.

Now, disturbed by her evening with Sed, Alex knelt and held the Bible talisman to her lips. She stared into a small hand-mirror and saw frightened eyes. She was a woman and attractive and an older married man had talked to her of love. She was a child and ashamed.

Still, the next day and the next, the game went on. He smiled relentlessly, and flattered, caressing the back of her neck as she filled salt-cellars in the storeroom, arranging her shifts so that they finished together, meeting secretly in the car park. And, still fearful, now she liked him enough to want not to hurt him, and that made it harder to think about stopping, even though she knew that while it was a delicious guilty game to her, it was not a game to him.

'That white Jew boy, he wants my wife. Well, he can keep her now I have you.'

'Don't say that, please.'

'But I want to marry you. I save hard. We both go to Persia. Is beautiful country. Beautiful, like you, like your poems.'

'Don't spoil it, Sed. This is silly talk. I'm too young to think about getting married, to anyone. I don't even want to get married, at least not for a long time. I told you, I'm going to be a reporter. And, please, you're hurting my arm . . .'

'In Persia, you not too young to be wife. You won't leave me, will you?'

The pleading of the feline brown eyes sobered her into silence and she let him kiss her with a passion she could not return.

Balmy July turned into August and all her excuses of 'having to work late' were making Dad suspicious.

'I'm not a schoolkid any more, Dad. I'm a working girl. And I can't always choose my hours to suit you. Anyway, you know it's only temporary. A newspaper job will turn up sooner or later. A weekly in Clevedon said they might give me an interview in September.'

But did she believe it? I don't know who I am, buzzed her head. Dead-end job and no prospects of anything different. No chance of escape from Stonebridge Road. Burdened – there was no other word for it. She felt crushed. There was a weight on her back pressing her down. Lines on her forehead. A child with a giant's backpack. An actress finding it hard to remember her words, losing her place on the page, longing for the final curtain. But surely the play had hardly begun?

Then one night the intimacy with Sed in the little van toppled into frightening new sensations. She panicked under the pressure of his hips, pushing hard against his jaw with her arm. A sob broke from her throat and he released her, his eyes confused and bleak.

'Sorry. Sorry,' she gasped, wrenching open the door. She ran into the embrace of a still, warm night.

An hour later, exhausted, she stood on the bridge and looked over. The River Avon was grey and dense, flecked with greasy foam. The temptation was there. She pictured herself, a doll floating downwards and being lost, swallowed, breaking. Following Mum and being with her for ever.

Her courage failed, giving her another reason to despise herself. She turned and walked to the bus stop, head bowed and hands in her pockets. She'd heard that history repeated itself. The lure of the water was strong, magnetic.

The boy van-driver had been easy to deal with. But this flesh-and-blood hurting man was different.

'The cook, she say you phone in yesterday and say you sick. You better now?'

Alex avoided his eyes.

'Yes, it was nothing much. I'm fine.'

'Hey, let's go for drive after work. You not look so happy. Sed make you very happy. OK?'

His enforced gaiety was tragic.

'No, not OK. I want to finish early and go to the Youth Employment Office.'

He looked crestfallen, bewildered.

'Look, you have to understand, Sed . . . I can't go on working here after the summer, and, well, I don't seem to be having much luck applying to newspapers. I want to go and have a chat with the Youth Employment people. Maybe I can do a course. Or something. I don't know. I need some advice.'

'You can stay here long as you like. I ask head office to give you rise. You very good worker, the best.'

'I don't know. That's not what I want. I don't know . . .' Her voice trailed off, miserably.

'My darling.'

'Don't call me that.'

'But, you don't understand. How much I need you, I . . .'

'No, you're the one that doesn't understand. Please don't need me!' she snapped back, her voice trembling and shrill, brutal.

The brown eyes stared, shocked. He turned. She grabbed his arm, sorry now.

'Don't go.'

He held her shoulders, the eyes now hopeful, trusting.

'Darling, Alex, you not well. OK. I tell you what we do. You go home early. Tomorrow everything normal, as usual. Tomorrow evening we take drive, eat shish kebab at my flat.'

'I've told you before, I don't think I should go to your flat. Ever.'

Weariness and misery gave her voice a hard, whining edge.

'Quiet, quiet. OK, my little angel. That's why I love you. You're so good. Good girl and good for Sed.'

'You don't know me at all. I'm not good.'

She finished work early, but didn't go home, or to the Youth Employment Office. A warm stifling evening. Walking again by the river, she saw the water tonight even more enticing, more blue than grey, lit with spangles of colour from the retreating sun. All that was needed was a second's courage followed by a minute's calm resignation and surrender. But she turned away.

The city was closing down. The flagstone square by the river scurried with office staff single-mindedly heading for their other lives. Reaching the pavement, they shifted their feet impatiently in the bus queue or strode towards the multi-storey car park, keys already jingling in their hands. Their eagerness for the next minute of being was an affront to her.

If only she could fade into nothingness: silently, effortlessly, rubbed out like an error on the blackboard. She made a mistake, or two or three, and needed to be erased. Blank.

Some time later, walking and worn out with her thoughts, Alex woke to the realization that she was in company with a different kind of crowd. A riverside pub was spilling out a loud flock of drinkers – a gang of rough shoving youths, a few older men unshaven and carrying raincoats and briefcases, one or two women wobbling on high heels, laughing dangerously.

Alex increased her pace, altering direction towards the

bus station. There was a rumble of thunder and a chill breeze swept by. She was in danger of missing the last bus. As she reached the kerb, she hesitated. Why this base instinct for survival? It didn't matter if she did miss the last bus.

As she stood there, the world flashed brightly, thunder cracked, and urgent drops of rain fell. Within seconds the kerbstones blackened and the rising wind was rank with summer dust. Within minutes the tarmac was glistening with reflected winking neon lights, blue and green and red, from the city centre's shining buildings, spelling *Prudential* and *Timex* and *Palace Theatre*. A welcome washing of tired streets. While she felt dirty.

Suddenly defiant, she lifted her face into the full force of the slanting, stinging storm. Closing her eyes, she stepped off the kerb and started walking steadily, surely. With cold deliberation. Yet, as in a dream. Far away she heard a jamming, grinding noise and the echo of a shouted curse. Three lanes of traffic, and she stumbled into the traffic island and its yellow bollard. Another three shrieking lanes and she reached the far kerb. Spared, she opened her eyes. Shaking her head in disbelief, she felt rivulets of rainwater creeping coldly down her neck and squeezing under her collar.

'You want the Common, luv? Hop on quick, you just made it. What a bastard of a night.'

The conductor took her fare, whistling, unassailably cheerful. Upstairs, the swaying floor was littered with the day's used tickets and cigarette butts. Almost deserted. Alex took the front seat, stared unseeing into the blackness of the steamy windows, and let the tears fall unchecked.

'Hello. Thought it was you. I almost missed it. Good thing it was late leaving tonight!'

Alex blinked hard and wiped her eyes with the back of her hand.

The girl squeezed in beside her, shaking an umbrella. The raindrops spotted her brown suede jacket. She reached into her handbag for a comb and ran it through her thick black hair. Alex recognized her. Judith? No, Jackie. She'd been at the same school, but had left after the fifth form to go to nursing college. She lived at Stancombe, a village a little distance beyond Stonepit Common.

'You look even more of a drowned rat than I do.' Jackie's voice was warm and sympathetic. Perhaps that was why Alex began to cry again.

Strangely, she didn't feel foolish. Just honest. She was intensely miserable and the tears were a natural expression. Life should always be that simple.

And soon, she was telling it all to Jackie, to an almost stranger. She told her about the pretend living, about being different people, about Sed, being trapped, wanting to die but being too afraid to let go, walking into the traffic but still being alive.

There was a healthy pink glow to Jackie's face that drew her on, an energy she could almost touch and compared with which Alex felt sickly pale. The truth fell from her with increasing confidence. But Jackie's response completely took her aback.

'Alex, you're in quite a mess and, honestly, I don't know what to say. I mean, I've got nothing to give you, not out of myself. But God can help you. And if you let him into your life, that could actually totally change everything.'

Alex remembered for ever that Jackie's eyes were alight as she reached into her handbag to draw out a small leather book.

Alex's pulse raced and her mouth felt dry. What had she

done? Had she told all this, opened up her heart, to some kind of religious freak? The resistance rose strong within her. But at the same time there was the comfort of remembering the way she looked on her own Bible as a talisman in the cupboard. That and Jackie's shining eyes. All these things conspired to persuade her to listen.

Jackie was turning the pages of the little New Testament, and lifting it up to Alex, balanced on the palm of her hand.

'. . . *casting all your care upon him, for he cares for you.* See that? See that promise? God said that. He said that you can give all your cares to him, whatever they are, because he cares for you.'

'No, no. You don't understand. The thing is, probably the very worst part of it all, is that no-one, no-one really does care for me. No-one. If I'd walked under one of those cars tonight, there wouldn't be a single . . .'

'That's where you're totally wrong. Totally. Do you know how much God loves you? He sent his only Son Jesus into this world to give his life, to die for you, so that you could have a new, a different life.'

'Look, I don't understand all this Jesus talk, and I really don't want to.'

Alex felt a reservoir of deep anger taking over then and wanted to hurt Jackie simply because she was so sure and happy. She raised a wall to her, yet hoped Jackie was strong enough to demolish it.

'It's just all so much simplistic rubbish. Gibberish. Crazy, this religion stuff. Actually, let me tell you something. I've tried, yes, I've really tried reading the Bible and it does nothing for me. Absolutely nothing. Just a fairy story. Forget it.'

Yet, Jackie was unshaken at her vehemence. And,

unaccountably, Alex discovered after all that she wanted to please the shining eyes. So she allowed her own reddened ones to dwell on the words Jackie was still holding out, underlining with her finger.

'. . . *casting all your care upon him, for he cares for you.*'

Alex let the words rise from the page, slowly parade through her mind and began to entertain them. And what if they *were* true? She'd never doubted there was a God, but his remote irrelevance gave him no more power than Julius Caesar or Henry VIII. Suppose, just suppose, that God was not only historically real, but interested.

'. . . *casting all your care upon him, for he cares for you.*'

The giant's backpack was there as always, pressing on her neck, the top of her spine. Yes, she had plenty of care. How tempting was the possibility that she could cast it away, throw it down, toss it away!

She bit her lip hard, then flashed a glance out of the black window.

'The next stop's mine.'

'Look, there's so much more to say. Come to chapel with me, this Sunday. I'll meet you here, your bus stop, at four o'clock. A crowd of us always have tea together first. Please come.'

Alex jerked to her feet and pressed the bell.

'I . . . I don't know. I'll have to think about it. Maybe. Don't count on it.'

The rain had stopped and so had her tears. She ran from the common along Stonebridge Road. Drowning, she'd been thrown a rope, but perhaps she was too suspicious of it fraying to grab it.

FIVE

Culture shock.

Years later, when people asked her if she experienced culture shock moving to Asia, Alex would say that, truthfully, no culture shock was greater than what she lived through during those few late summer months when she was eighteen. Translated from the kingdom of darkness to the kingdom of light – that's the way she found it described in the Bible and that's the way it was. She stumbled into another country. And it all started the first Sunday evening she went with Jackie to the Evangelical Chapel.

Alex allowed herself a smile, lying in the bath at the cottage.

Another full day of work. She was tired and tense. She contemplated the energy needed to launch into painting the kitchen now that the sitting-room walls were complete. She imagined the sitting-room warmed with russet carpet and bright with curtains. Curtains. She must call the freight company. Her packing cases should arrive soon.

She examined her hands. The fingers were sore, knuckles

scraped, nails ragged with chips of paint and filler. Busy. But empty. These days her hands always looked empty.

Did the Evangelical Chapel still stand? Still exercise its vigorous witness to the resisting working-class city suburb that surrounded it? Suddenly, the need to know was as desperate as a crumbling handhold in a rockface.

The next day was a Saturday. She knocked on Helen's door, a bulging holdall at her feet.

'Hi! Only me,' she said, with nervous brightness. 'Could I take you up on the offer of using your washing-machine? If it's convenient, that is. Don't worry if it . . .'

'Come in, Alex. Of course. Can you stay for coffee?'

Helen's cottage home was a larger, more modern version of Alex's. Waiting for the coffee machine to complete its bubbling, Alex found herself looking around appreciatively at the tiles and pine units.

'I sometimes feel I've bitten off more than I can chew with our . . . my cottage. But it's something we'd planned to do, you know . . . together . . . before . . . all this happened. I can't feel I can settle to anything else till it's done. I think I'll have to get some professional help with one or two bits, though. Like the stairs. I can't work out how I could possibly do the ceiling and walls where the stairs turn. It's quite a height there.'

They chatted, nibbled shortbread, sipped coffee. Neighbourly. Conversation was slow, as if an engine long shut down needed coaxing into full-steamed compliance. They kept to safe ground, swapped DIY hints, expressed concern for local education cuts, shared anxiety over the speed of lorries through the village. Then there was the media's fascination with the new Prince Harry, and the Queen's tour of Canada. Helen's daughter's fascination with Boy George. Helen's disillusion with the miner's leader Arthur

Scargill now that he was involved in a court case. The effrontery of ITV's hit puppet show *Spitting Image*. The scandal of the unemployment figures being their highest ever. Alex stuttered, stumbled, brushed crumbs into little heaps on the chequered tablecloth, hard-pressed to be fluent. She had been unused for months to such social niceties as coffee conversation. And she felt embarrassed that as a journalist she should be so out of touch with current events.

'Before I forget, is there any chance you have a decent road map I could borrow? Mine's useless, it's so out of date.'

Helen fetched a book from the lounge.

'This year's, no less. Sarah gave it to me for Christmas. Borrow it for as long as you like.'

'I only need it for tomorrow. It's a long time since I went to Bristol, I need to check the route.'

'Planning a day out?'

'Not exactly. Well, sort of, but . . . Helen, I don't suppose . . . If you were free tomorrow, would you be interested in coming? Just sitting here with you, well, makes me realize how nice it is to have a bit of intelligent conversation, you know.'

'Flattered, I'm sure.' Helen laughed. 'Well, let me see. I've a stack of essays to mark but I could get that done this evening. I'm expected tomorrow for stewarding at early communion, but I'm free afterwards. I could be with you by ten thirty. Would that do?'

Mild for early October, Sunday dawned bright and promising. Soon after eleven Alex was cautiously easing the Metro down the slip-road on to the M4 outside Swindon.

'Why do they have to make road systems so complic-ated?'

'Traffic's increased quite a bit in five years.'

'And got faster! I can hardly believe this is the *slow* lane.'

'Well, I guess a lot's changed while you've been away. Reverse culture shock, don't they call it?'

There were one or two wrong moves once inside the city, but Alex was surprised how familiar it was, how relatively effortlessly they drew up alongside a low wall, over which squatted a grey stone chapel building. It was plain, very plain. On one side a terrace of houses with small front gardens stretched away into the distance; on the other stood a petrol station and car-wash.

'It's years since I've been here. The petrol station's new. Used to be a newsagent's. And a shoe-repairer's, I think. Everything else looks much the same, I suppose. The church looks smaller, sort of greyer. More neglected.'

'So this is where you and Peter . . .'

'Yes,' she interrupted, rather too curtly. 'This is where . . . where everything, really.'

Helen squinted into the pale sunshine.

'According to the notice board, the morning service must be over. But there's some kind of women's meeting on this afternoon. Two o'clock. We could find somewhere a bit more picturesque to eat our sandwiches and come back later. If you'd like to see inside?'

'Would you mind?'

But as Alex reached for the ignition, they saw an elderly man in flat cap and navy raincoat walking purposefully up to the arched door of the chapel, holding a key.

'Come on,' said Helen, already half out of her seat. 'We might be able to get a private viewing.'

The flat cap nodded. 'Just a few minutes, though. I shan't be long downstairs.'

The caretaker had come to check the heating clock for

the afternoon meeting, but let them into the main hall while he slipped through a side door to deal with the boiler.

Hard, almost impossible, to see the chapel again through youthful uninitiated eyes, without the wisdom of hindsight. Motionless, Alex stared over the untidy rows of wooden chairs. And struggled to recall that long-ago overwhelming sensation of having fallen like Alice in Wonderland down a rabbit tunnel into another world.

'Take the seat at the end of the front row and keep the next one for me while I fetch some hymnbooks! I'll introduce you to everyone afterwards,' Jackie had said.

The young Alex sat stiffly and stared straight ahead, conscious of a growing volume of greetings and laughter behind her, shuffling of feet on bare floorboards, scraping of chair legs. It all sounded a bit irreligious. She had taken in only the briefest impressions as Jackie ushered her in through a side door, but she felt uneasy. No stained glass or candles. No pews or scent of polish. No comforting shadows. Before her stood a small, unadorned table and beyond that a raised area some three or four feet high, skirted by a rail and a blue velvet curtain. The wall above was painted with flowing script: *Worship the Lord in the Beauty of Holiness*.

Jackie arrived with half a dozen chattering, giggling girls who filled up most of the front row. One thrust a hymnbook into her hand. Two others carried tambourines embellished with trailing multicoloured ribbons, which they slid noisily under their chairs.

Church or carnival? Alex's bewilderment grew as the service progressed. A small balding man in a grey suit, with the rosy cheeks of a gypsy, crooked teeth and an infectious grin, performed a role she thought of more as master of ceremonies than minister of religion. Any resemblance to the hushed solemnity of St John's would be hard to find. The singing was energetic, raucous even, and punctuated with spirited interruptions of 'Hallelujah!' or 'Amen, brother!' At the end of a hymn someone read out a few lines and the athletic young man at the piano led off into a breathless repeat rendition of the whole six verses again. The two girls with the tambourines faced everyone at the front, their instruments trilling and dancing in flounces and flashing figures of eight.

A young woman in a knitted cap sang a quavering solo. Then the red-cheeked man asked for a 'testimony' and a middle-aged man leapt to his feet and told the congregation that God had healed him of a slipped disc after he was prayed for the previous Sunday. Someone else came forward to 'bring a word from the Lord'.

Alex began to lose a grip on things. Half hoping to find some answers, instead she was overwhelmed with questions. *'Casting all your care . . .'*

The service had ended with a quiet, soulful hymn which prompted three of the congregation to kneel at the front, heads bowed, while others gathered around to pray for them, arms outstretched. Even before this was over, a blessing was pronounced and the hall erupted into excited chatter, while two women materialized on cue from a side door, carrying metal trays of teacups.

'Not much to see, is there?' commented Helen, acidly, raising critical brows. 'I've been in corner shops with more interesting architecture. Scruffy too.'

Alex, roused from her reverie, was suddenly defensive.

'All a matter of what you're used to. You've been at St Matthew's for years, haven't you? They worship the same God here, you know. Even without all the quaint carving and lamps and everything. Plenty of people would say, and I think they've got a good point, that all that is simply pretty packaging. Not needed.'

She walked to the front and fingered the wooden table. The same wooden table.

'See these worn floorboards here? No embroidered kneeler or carpet. But this is the spot where I knelt for the most significant minutes of my life. And where Peter and I . . .' Her eyes blurred and she looked away.

'Sorry,' muttered Helen, arriving alongside and awkwardly taking her arm. 'Don't take any notice of me. I can be a cynical, thoughtless bitch. Come on. The caretaker's waiting for us. Let's go back to the car. I want you to tell me all about it.'

'I'm sorry, for over-reacting. I don't really know if I can talk. Yes, we'd better go. There's a nice peaceful park a couple of streets away, or used to be. Let's drive there.'

They found a sheltered bench in a curve of thick shrubbery next to a lake.

Alex took a deep breath.

How could she make Helen – or anyone – understand what it was like for her to find herself in the chapel? A mixed-up kid from a council estate who'd hardly ever set foot in a church?

'My background, well, it's so different from yours,' she began. 'Didn't you tell me once you were third generation at St Matthew's?'

Helen nodded, unpacking the flask and sandwiches.

'Yes. Grandad was organist there for over thirty years, Dad sang in the choir as a boy, and until her hip operation Mum was a leading light on every committee you could name. Sue and I were brought up to go twice to church every Sunday, without fail. Sue got rebellious in her teenage years and took her chance to move away from the village and the church as soon as she could. But somehow I've stuck at it. Trevor and I were married at St Matthew's and when our relationship floundered it was the church people who really helped me. In fact, they were the ones that stood by me when the rest of the village were gossiping behind my back about Trevor's . . . his indiscretions, as Mum so quaintly puts it.'

Helen flushed and bit into a ham sandwich.

'All water under the bridge,' she went on, more briskly. 'But I suppose I'd never thought that deeply about my faith, just blindly accepted it, until I hit that awful patch. It made a lot more sense from then on, though I'm far from having all the answers. Must be a lot of people like me, brought up in the church and not really discovering what it's all about until they're up to their necks in a crisis and then . . .'

'True. But, Helen,' Alex interrupted, 'there are just as many people out there – no, *more* – living in a crisis and *not* having a clue that there's any way out at all, and with no more than a faint skirmish into faith in their backgrounds, if that.'

'Go on. Is that where you were?'

'In my mid and late teens I felt weighed down with so many things. Looking back, I have this mental picture of me with the face of a child, but horribly bent over like a wizened old woman, with a heavy sack on her back. A chip on my shoulder, and how! I felt quite bitter about things, some of which I couldn't change. A lot of what was wrong in my life was wrong because of me, though, and deep down I knew it and I needed to take the blame, but couldn't.'

Helen held out a cup brimming with coffee. 'Sorry to be

rather disparaging, but I can't see how coming to this, this chapel could help you. If what you needed was to find some help in religion . . .?' She shrugged, uneasily.

'Go on, say it! What had this tin tabernacle to offer me? I understand why you'd say that, why you'd think your own church tradition so much . . . much richer. But I was a million miles away from conventional church life, with all sorts of hang-ups about it. Anything I'd seen of the church was so cluttered with outdated ceremonial, it meant nothing to me. I couldn't get through the barrier of all that.

'The chapel was different. Incredibly different! I was scared. Overwhelmed, at first. Out of my depth. It was another language, another culture. But it was the culture shock I needed to face up to the basic issues – my need of being rescued from the mess I'd made of my life. I needed God. The preaching at the chapel had a directness which shook me. Even the singing was different. We sang these simple, moving Moody and Sankey hymns which touched something frozen deep down inside and melted me into tears. I began to make sense of it and, more amazing, it began to make sense of me! It was believing in all the same things you and all the people at St Matthew's believe in. But it was believing with . . . with the walls down.'

'You've lost me. What do you mean, with the walls down?'

'Well, the kind of formalized religion I'd glimpsed here and there always seemed to be behind walls, to need its own interpreter. The vicar or priest or whoever – he played that role to the congregation, trying to translate what faith was all about into words they could understand, so that they received it in a sort of secondhand way.'

Helen protested. 'Hey, it's not like that, not like that at all.'

67

'Sorry, perhaps now *I'm* being cynical. But I'm trying to remember what I thought back then, as far as I thought about it at all. Maybe I'm wrong. Perhaps the churchgoers I saw all had a real faith. But, if so, it seemed some kind of closely guarded secret. Because quite honestly a lot of them *acted* as if all they had was a secondhand faith – removed from them, not quite relevant. Certainly not something they talked about.'

'Look, not everyone wants to be so . . . so demonstrative about what they believe,' said Helen. 'Me included. That's not to say we *don't* believe.'

'Of course not!' Alex smiled. 'I know that *now*. But when you're struggling to know something, anything at all, then you can only go on what you can see. And Jackie and all her friends – they all had something very much up front, first-hand. It showed. They talked about God and Jesus and the Holy Ghost as if they were real, intimately known to them. Like especially close friends. Or like . . . like lovers. Does that sound a bit sacrilegious to you?'

'Maybe. Well, yes, I suppose it does.'

'I'll be honest – that was my first reaction, too. Along with the thought that they were all so very complacent to be talking about mysterious holy things in ordinary down-to-earth language. As if they had some privileged position with the Almighty. Their certainties attracted, yet at the same time bothered me for quite some time, I can tell you. I remember thinking how incredibly . . . presumptuous they all were! What Jackie and her friends had weren't the kind of trembling vague hopes I thought religion offered. They told me it was possible to be definite, to have *certainty* about lots of things, even huge things like knowing God.'

'Certainty. Now there's a word to conjure with,' said Helen, sighing heavily.

They sat silently, two women staring out across the lake, at sea in separate pasts. A solitary swan emerged from the reeds in the distance, setting off ripple rings that gently extended, widening, till they lapped the edge close to their bench.

'Maybe that's the real thing I found at the chapel,' Alex began again slowly. 'Certainty. Because after listening to them and hearing a confidence that bordered on . . . well, I don't know . . . sheer cheek it seemed at first! But after that, I was able to get out my old Bible and read it in an entirely different way. This time I didn't get bogged down in rituals of animal sacrifice. Jackie showed me how to get straight into the Gospels and find out about Jesus. God in the shape of man. God's way of making his mysterious self known to man. I found the same certainty there that I found in my new friends and their rather excitable services. Like an echo. It gave me something solid to build my life on.'

Helen sighed. 'Come on, shall we go?'

Alex glanced quickly at her.

'Helen, have I offended you? I didn't mean to be so critical of St Matthew's and everything. And I don't want to undervalue traditional ways of doing things. It's just that for me . . .'

Helen stood up abruptly and threw the crust of her sandwich into the water. 'I'm sure you don't mean to make me feel this, but I feel kind of guilty to be part of that traditional church life that didn't touch you, couldn't reach you. Not only that, if I'm honest I almost feel jealous of that experience you had. It sounds as if it had quite an impact on your life.'

Impact! Culture shock! Alex's world held its breath, waiting to somersault, land upside down . . .

SIX

It began to rain heavily. Alex closed the windows, locked and bolted the doors against the smell of bonfire smoke and wet leaves. Dusk fell earlier and earlier, and dawn lingered mercilessly.

She reflected miserably on her self-imposed exile. The time spent on the renovation each day seemed to extend, while progress shrank and was frustrating. At some indefinable point her well-constructed plans had drifted alarmingly into daily aimlessness.

It was so cold she no longer stood in the overgrown walled garden watching the petals fall from the late wild roses. And anyway her imagination had begun to people its leafy shadows with unnamed threats. She had bought a cheap radio to give her voices in the emptiness, but the endless political wrangling and aggressive panel discussions grated, and she settled for light fluffy music.

Tonight her head and her hand throbbed.

Somehow she had assumed the role of recluse. She hadn't meant to. Each evening she resolved that tomorrow she would go into the village, meet people. She must phone Mandy. And invite Helen for a meal to thank her for coming on the trip to Bristol. But after another night ravaged by nightmares, each new morning found her dispirited. She had even driven to an anonymous super-market in Oxford and stocked up with food supplies to avoid a trip to the village minimart. Her cowardice was not a surprise, reminiscent as it was of the times she had drawn back from the river. It was just that she had thought that was all in the past.

Homecomings. They always held so much promise, but were often disillusioning, deflating. She thought of Peter's homecomings to the flat in Hong Kong, his return from those many trips when she'd stayed behind and he'd gone to Bangkok or Manila or Bombay, for two, maybe three, maybe four weeks. The prime joy was in the anticipation of his homecoming. Dropping into the office to see if there was a fax on the machine with a coded postscript. Phoning the airline to check if the flight was on time. Just simply thinking of news and experiences to be shared, stories to be told, thinking of open arms and cool sheets and rediscovery of that other part of self that had been missing like an amputated limb.

Sometimes the reality matched the dream. But often the anticipation was, in truth, more wonderful than the reality. Because there was the hard fact of the traveller's baggage. Not just the suitcase full of crumpled clothing and unfinished reports with threatening deadlines. But the dark shadows under the glazed eyes, stifled yawns, aching feet, swollen mosquito bites, the kidnapped aroma of faraway street refuse mingling on his skin with the stale smoke of other travellers' cigarettes.

And what of the traveller's wife? The anticipation was

that she would be waiting, pretty in some light cotton dress or sensuous in some silk dressing-gown. Well, sometimes that might be true. But at other times she would be resentful at being left with the stress of some domestic or office crisis, however trivial, that must be endured and conquered alone. And having steeled herself to deal solitarily with the world she might still be impregnable, defensive. And the barriers dissipated only slowly with continuing gentle companionship.

Yes, homecomings so often failed to be as sweet as they should be.

Alex stared around the kitchen, which tonight felt claustrophobic. She had repainted the ceiling and two of the walls. She needed to remove a shelf from the wall over the sink before she could continue. The only screwdriver she found in the shed was too small, and in wrestling with the rusted screws that afternoon it had slipped and badly gashed her left hand, now bathed and wrapped in a piece of an old towel.

Probably there were more tools in the loft. If she could find a bigger screwdriver tonight, it would save time tomorrow. And while she was up in the loft she would find her recipe books and plan a supper to which she would invite Helen. And there was that box of scrapbooks she wanted to get down.

Moving boxes around in the dim light of a single bulb and with a bandaged hand was not easy. Crawling into the far corner, she found Peter's rusting metal toolbox which, though small, was heavy. As she lifted it, her knee slipped on the edge of a rafter and, automatically reaching down to save herself, she felt a searing pain as the damaged hand took her weight. She let out a yelp. At the same time, the toolbox slipped from her grasp and fell about a foot. There was an ominous crack.

Alex was angry with her own clumsiness. Imprisoned under the toolbox was something wrapped in several layers of newspaper. She pulled out broken fragments of cream pottery. She punched at the rafter with her one good hand and howled.

'Well, this *has* to be our most wonderful wedding present to date!'

Alex remembered instantly how she had laughed out loud as she had pulled it from the floral paper.

Peter had snatched it up and threw his arm around her.

'Now, don't be like that, *Mrs* Davis! Uncle Tom means well. I told you he's a bit eccentric. I'll fill it with red roses and it'll look very romantic on the sideboard next to that shocking pink knitted tea-cosy from whichever one of *your* relatives produced that!'

The cream pottery vase represented a chubby fish standing on its tail, waiting for a bouquet to pop into its open mouth.

'Everyone's been so generous to us.'

She surveyed the jumble of silver ribbons and rumpled wrapping paper spilling from the kitchen table on to the floor.

'It's all a dream,' she whispered, closing her eyes.

'No, my love, it's for real,' said Peter, taking her hand and pressing it to his lips.

'Local girl makes good,' she murmured.

'What?'

'Today's headline. Or tomorrow's fairy tale.'

'Talking of happy endings, isn't this where we ride off into the sunset? Come with me, princess . . .'

A honey of a honeymoon cottage. Where once dreams came true. Where now nightmares ruled.

Alex swept the pottery shards to one side with her foot and cautiously felt her way back to the loft opening and down the ladder with the toolbox, making a return trip for the scrapbooks. Breaking the jug had upset her unreasonably. What were a few more broken pieces? Once before all the fragments had come together, renewed. Why couldn't it happen now?

Culture shock. Coming together. Renewal.

Following her early visits to the chapel, there had been a period of inner wrestling that went on for weeks. Intimidation gave way to reluctant admiration for Jackie and her friends. Brash they might be, but they possessed something real that Alex longed for. That certainty, that confidence in a God who cared for them, that assurance that there was more than the visible and tangible. She flirted dangerously with the new ideas, but as yet without commitment.

Life at Chico's began to look different.

'Sed, I really *do* need a bit of space. I *do* need to get my life straightened out. I feel like I've somehow got off the track, or maybe I never really found it. I'm taking tomorrow morning off. I've made an appointment with a Careers Officer.'

He shrugged, and regarded her suspiciously from the high stool at the till.

'You know what I think?' His voice was tense, quietly hissing. 'What I think, you have new boyfriend. You make the fool of me. These new friends you tell me about, this funny church club you go to, one of them . . .'

'No, believe me, there's no-one else. I would tell you.'

She could say no more. Her lips tasted of betrayal.

The next day, nervous and nail-biting, she dressed in the pale blue woollen trouser-suit she'd bought with several weeks' wages, and brushed her long brown hair back under a band of ribbon.

Nothing to lose, she decided, kneeling on impulse by her bed in the boxroom. Jackie kept telling her that prayer was just like talking with a friend you loved, only more.

'God, please stop me from being nervous. And please let there be a job for me. Even if there's only one, let it be the one, and I'll take it. Anything for a new start.' She wished it sounded more profound.

She ran down the stairs two at a time. Dad was at the kitchen table, the *Daily Mirror* propped behind a mug of tea. He'd not been in long from the night shift.

'Bye, Dad. I'm off now. Wish me luck.'

'You look a right bobby dazzler in that outfit. Must 'ave cost a packet! Off you go and don't be late for yer 'pointment. You can't rely on them buses, they'm goin' from bad to worse.' He dismissed her with a wave.

When the form-filling was over, there was a long wait in reception until she was ushered into a cluttered office.

An elderly man was stooping over the middle drawer of a filing cabinet.

'Sit down, Miss . . . umm. Well, I've had a look through your exam results, interests, umm, so on. Can't give you much encouragement as far as the aspirations to journalism are concerned, though. Very competitive, you know.' He looked at her over his glasses, quizzical. She returned the stare as boldly as she dared.

He pulled out a file and spread it on the table in front of her.

'I've got one opening here might be of interest, and I'm afraid it *is* the only one at present.'

Alex took a deep breath. Her morning prayer had been

so simple. 'Even if there's only one, let it be the one, and I'll take it.'

The man passed her a form and pointed to the address at the top.

'There's an advertising agency just off Chatsworth Square wanting someone to operate a photographic dark-room in their design studio. Pay's a bit on the low side. Training will be given to a suitable applicant. Asking for a boy, actually, as you'll see from the form there. A boy with an interest in photography.'

He laughed, apologetically.

'But the request's been here several weeks with no takers, so I might be able to twist their arm to give you an interview, even if you don't quite fit the bill. Interested?'

Dazed, she found herself nodding. She didn't even own a camera.

Was it the bedside prayer that let her into the advertising studio? Like the house that Jack built, one thing led to another. This, then, was the prayer, the prayer that got the job, the job that found the man, the man that won the heart, the heart that broke in pieces, the pieces of the jug, the jug that lay in the loft, in the loft of the honeymoon cottage.

The love that drew her to Peter had an inevitability about it. But magical, all the same. Like a spell cast over them both, only to be shattered years later when the grey wall entombed him.

Peter, too, had been poised on the brink of a new direction when she met him at the advertising agency. However, unlike her, all that was behind him urged him to look up, not down.

Orphaned at an age before recall, Peter had the good fortune to be raised by two bachelor uncles whose positive, carefree outlook on life exhaled an infectious if slapdash enthusiasm.

Leaving their chaotic Staffordshire household after a couple of years in a mediocre local art school, Peter had found the job as a junior paste-up artist in Bristol. Somehow the departure of the young man sent the two uncles into a swift decline. Gerald, the exuberant elder, had succumbed to a lung cancer which claimed his life within months. Tom, always so quiet and calm, was overnight confused and distressed. He abruptly sold the family home. Suddenly grey and shrunken, he moved into a tiny flat in a sheltered housing project. He insisted that Peter take as his own the country cottage the brothers owned in Oxfordshire and to which they had happily transported him each school holiday for years.

Uncle Gerald's sudden death hit Peter hard. Instinctively he felt the best tribute to his stand-in father was to face the threatening loneliness with cheerfulness.

However, it was a time for reflection. Gerald and Tom had been Catholics all their lives and now it seemed to Peter that many of his memories of the two men were inextricably linked with their folksy, rather superstitious religion. They attended Mass irregularly yet made no overt attempt to pass on their faith to Peter, but he began to realize how much he'd taken on board by a strange osmosis.

Peter found himself recalling with amusement a familiar scene in the untidy house. He would be dashing around looking for an elusive history textbook he needed for school that day, throwing aside cushions, scattering old newspapers and the Sunday supplements Tom insisted on keeping in knee-high stacks around the kitchen. Tom himself would be buttering toast and pressing it into Peter's hand. 'Now, it would be a disgrace if I was to let you go off without a proper breakfast on a perishin' morning like today.' Gerald, meanwhile, would be theatrically intoning a prayer to St Anthony, his eyes heavenward, while sucking on his pipe. 'He's the patron saint of all lost things. Don't they teach you that at school, then?'

Was there anything in that religion stuff? In recent months, noticeably since his uncle's death, Peter's work at the advertising studio left him dissatisfied, hungry for significance. The campaigns he worked on to press dishwashers, whisky and sports cars, bank loans and timeshares on the great British public were at best shallow, at worst smutty, he decided. He felt a longing for the old holiday cottage, and scanned the 'situations vacant' columns for jobs in Oxfordshire.

With so much restlessness in the air, Alex's arrival in the advertising studio, and the disturbing impact she had on him, only added to his confusion.

'I'm only here temporarily. Until I get a job on a newspaper.' Her voice was wary.

He grinned. 'I might be only temporary, too. And I was only suggesting a coffee after work. What's the matter? Is there a boyfriend?'

She winced, remembering the crumpling of Sed's olive face.

'No. Not right now. OK. Friday, then?'

Perversely, the more the magnetism worked on them, the more they aided and abetted the wrenching apart.

'Have you written off about that trainee reporter vacancy on the weekly yet?'

'Here's my draft letter. Tell me what you think. And what about you? Have you thought any more about that course in Oxford?'

'I've got an interview. It's a big step. If they ask me why I'm changing careers, what can I tell them?'

'The truth. Say you're disillusioned with the rat race. Want to do something meaningful. Working with people. You know the kind of thing.'

Alex got the job on the weekly. And then the inevitable happened.

'Great! I knew you could do it! When does the course begin?' Was her voice trembling?

'Six weeks from Monday. And the grant's come though. I think I'll hand in my notice tomorrow. But . . . how can I . . .'

He crushed her hard to his chest, questions hanging like rainclouds over their heads.

The prospect of not seeing each other every day forced them to admit the unspoken longing to be together. They began to meet at every opportunity in the weeks left to them, before Peter departed for life in a countryside cottage, commuting to Oxford for a personnel management course, and Alex remained in Bristol, now well launched into her early days as a trainee reporter.

'Thursday evenings I usually meet up with some friends, at a sort of church youth group.'

'Great. I'll come along.'

She hesitated. 'You might not like it. It's . . . well, judge for yourself.'

She was quite unprepared for the enthusiasm with which Peter threw himself into the meetings and long discussions with her new friends afterwards.

'There's a guest evangelist next Sunday evening, Lexa. I told Jackie we'd be there.'

'I thought we were going to that new pub by the river, the one advertising live jazz.'

'We can go there any time, can't we?'

But they never did go there. And now they never would. No matter.

Nursing her aching hand, Alex curled up on the sofa with the box of scrapbooks.

'New record for doughnut-eating champ.' 'Bypass protest march halts traffic.' 'School blaze: police suspect arson.'

She slowly turned the pages. The yellow newspaper cuttings pasted into the cheap scrapbooks were not just the record of a local community, but part of her own personal history. Hardly Fleet Street. But from the start she was devoted to the *Kingsfield Sentinel*, the rather old-fashioned weekly on which she served her three years indentures, with its district news roundup, its formulaic obituaries, its rows of wedding reports with photos framed in bells and ribbons. Rates rises or surveys on juggernaut traffic made the banner headlines. Inside pages were stuffed with the minutiae of little happenings: church fetes, fire-station open days, amateur dramatic society productions of Gilbert and Sullivan, school netball team triumphs.

'Names and faces. Names and faces. That's what sells a local rag! Now you get out there and write me some more names and faces,' thundered Will Hastings, the corpulent sub-editor who had oversight of the reporting team of four. He presided over the Monday morning editorial meetings with an odd mixture of good humour and tyranny, dirty thumbs tucked into red braces stretched over an expanse of chest.

'Alex, I'm chucking that finance committee preview right back on your desk because it's plain bloody boring. And about 300 words too long. Get on to Councillor Evans and spice it up with a few quotes. Live dangerously. And I want you at that inquest with Andy this afternoon writing a shadow report – damn good experience for a young hack like you. Tomorrow you can cover that soap star opening the show house on the Northwold estate. See if you can dig up some juicy questions on her love life, or failing that give us a blow-by-blow account of what fashionable outfit the tart's wearing, and we can use it on the women's page next week. Book somebody to take pics. And where's that write-up on double glazing I asked you to do for the DIY spread?'

Voices from the past rose like heady incense from the scrapbook pages. Days of adventure. Released from Stone-bridge Road, she explored the independence of living in the flat at The Baulk, the excitement of intoxicating weekends with Peter. There was a new richness about life that gave her confidence. The *Sentinel* gave her a longed-for identity. 'I'm from the *Sentinel*' opened doors, and she felt dazzled by her own small successes: Will's occasional beam of commendation, the by-line in type however small, the nod of recognition from reporters of loftier publications in the corridors of the magistrates' courts. She no longer walked by the riverside. But . . .

But there were times when she was aware that the past was still a burden on her back, that her child's face was still lined with regrets, that doubt and depression lurked uneasily only just offstage. The kind of indefinable guilt that always shadowed her was not that easily erased.

SEVEN

The St Matthew's choir, some dozen middle-aged women in blue gowns, were stumbling to the finale of a showy piece in Latin.

Alex, wondering at the aspirations of a village church choirmaster, let her mind loose, eyes ranging over the stone pillars and vaulted ceiling. The stained-glass windows above the altar, predominantly red and blue, glowed warmly with the influence of a wan October sun. The centrepiece was a bleeding lamb. The lamb that takes away the sins of the world.

Surprising, really, she was reflecting, that the word 'guilt' appeared only a couple of times in the Bible. And those few references were mainly buried in a section of Deuteronomy setting down rules for dealing with murderers. Yet it, guilt that is, was such a common human experience.

Seated next to her, Helen leaned forward in the pew, hands clasped, eyes closed, face intent and, Alex had to admit, serene. Her lips moved in private communication.

Alex felt a pang of sorrow over the intimacy of prayer that she had abruptly lost and then mostly denied herself for months past. The grey wall had cut her off. A temporary loss? It had to be. She ached for its return, knew the initiative was hers, yet remained stubborn.

Somehow she never felt at home in St Matthew's. It was the only church in the village, so she and Peter had made an effort to attend after their marriage. But they were impatient with the time it took to get to know people there, and often, dragging their heels at the Sunday breakfast table, would decide on the spur of the moment to drive to Bristol, arriving at the chapel breathless during the opening singing. They knew they were themselves partly to blame for their difficulty in settling. They felt guilty about their divided loyalties. And maybe it was guilt that had brought her along this morning.

'For whoever shall keep the whole law, and yet stumble in one point, he is guilty of all.' The vicar's words, slow, sonorous, floated down from the lectern to rest on her. Alex felt uncomfortable at his apparent eavesdropping on her private world.

Guilty of all. That's what she came to see at the chapel, the truth that finally explained the pressing burden on her back. A tendency to tell lies and a yielding to shoplifting hardly qualified her for a 'wanted' poster. But she recognized herself, in common with everyone, stumbling on many points and therefore, by a higher reckoning, guilty of all. Guilty in God's eyes and separated from him. The human condition without salvation.

Separated, that is, until one particular long-past but not long-lost Sunday evening.

The chapel had been packed that evening, the fluorescent orange posters having attracted a number of curious newcomers from the estate. Peter was bubbly, joking and jostling with Jackie and the others. Alex watched, feeling detached and slightly resentful about sharing him. He was driving to Oxfordshire after the service to start his course the following day.

That same bleeding lamb was the theme of the guest speaker's message. His words were compelling, urgent. And so direct they pierced her already wounded heart.

'Dear ones, I don't want to know what you've done – specifically. I already know you've done wrong, as we all have. We've all come short of God's standard. That heaviness you feel, your troubled conscience, is simply telling you exactly that. You need the forgiveness that God sent his Son into the world to explain and provide.' The voice was honeyed but not insincere.

As Alex listened, the jigsaw pieces of recent months began to assemble into a beautiful picture. Tantalizingly incomplete but lovely. Snippets of Bible verses, phrases from old hymns, echoes of conversations – all dovetailed, interlocked, connected. She glimpsed a seamless truth.

Under the revelation, her heart thumped violently, her palms sweating, her mouth so dry she couldn't sing the last hymn. Her feet felt floating and numb, giving no contact with the earth. She was feverish with the excitement of coming over the crest of a hill to a crossroads and knowing the choice of direction was life-changing.

The preacher's voice broke in, loud and insistent, before the last soft notes of the hymn. She knew without doubt that she wanted what he was offering. She pushed her way along the row, eyes unseeing, and fell to her knees alongside the wooden table. She did not notice that Peter, too, was making his way to the front.

Within minutes a transaction was effected in her heart

and mind and soul, earth to heaven, heaven to earth. When she rose to her feet, awkward and trembling as a new-birthed foal, she rose as a new creation. Inwardly, she possessed the kernel of a rock-like confidence in God, invading her, possessing her with a deep sense of peace. Outwardly, she lifted her head with an airy lightness, sensing with surprise and joy the absence of the near-physical burden of her past. Most dramatically, she felt clean and new. She was born again.

'Ready to go?'

'Oh, yes! Sorry, Helen! I was miles away.'

'You looked it.'

Helen and Alex emerged from the low porch into the overgrown and sodden churchyard. To the right of the path Alex glimpsed fresh clods of earth piled around a newly dug grave. She shivered.

'Winter's definitely in the air,' Helen remarked.

Alex remained silent.

'I'm so glad the vicar slotted in those prayers for the government. Some escape for the Iron Lady, wasn't it!'

Alex admitted she was only barely aware of the week's big news story. What was happening to her, to the reporter in her? Brighton's Grand Hotel rocked by an IRA bomb and she was unmoved. Only not entirely. Picking up fragments of the news on the radio, she had tried to imagine what it would have been like to have Peter pulled from the debris, like the politician's wife, alive but paralysed. She knew she wouldn't have been much good as a nurse to an invalid. But to have him alive even though disabled . . .

When would she be able to be objective again? Not interpret events in the lopsided light of her individual and private tragedy?

Back at the cottage, Alex took jacket potatoes and a chicken casserole from the oven.

'I hope the potatoes are cooked through. We hardly ate potatoes at all in Asia – too expensive and mostly poor quality. I'm more at home cooking rice.'

Helen was an appreciative guest, and Alex soon relaxed and didn't need to be apologetic. She was warmed by the meal and by her company. Afterwards they sat in the redecorated sitting-room, drinking coffee. Helen admired the colour scheme and the batik throw-over that brightened the old sofa. On an impulse, Alex took out one of the albums that were stacked in the corner and flicked through the pages.

'Here. The batik's made in this workshop that SaveAid runs for ex-mental patients. It's in a sprawling city called Bogor, about an hour's drive from Jakarta – or three if it's during the rush hour. Oxford Circus has nothing on Jakarta, believe me!

'This is Hasoloan, who manages the marketing and sales. And Soen, a lovely man – he's retired and travels over from Bandung to be a kind of part-time counsellor for the workers.'

Alex chattered on, excited, almost intoxicated. The photographs represented a world of people and places she'd kept rigidly at arm's length for months. But now the memories came tumbling back, fresher than yesterday, brighter than paint.

And the pain when she spoke about her love was even bearable.

'Of course, Peter had absolutely no idea what the personnel management course would lead to, but without that he would never have considered applying for the job at the Oxford HQ of SaveAid. He worked there for . . . just over six years, it would have been, as the assistant to the director who recruits staff for the overseas aid projects. And then, incredibly, Peter was asked to consider going to manage some of the projects in Asia. They knew I was a reporter. By then I'd finished my indentures at the *Kingsfield Sentinel* and moved on to the *North Wilts Gazette*. And they asked me if I'd write for them part-time – reports and interviews that they could use in the fund-raising materials.'

'So off you set from Oxfordshire to the other side of the world. I'm not sure I could have done that!'

'Well, yes. Not entirely anxiety-free. Peter's Uncle Tom was frail, and promises of regular letters weren't enough to stop him getting quite upset at the thought of losing the monthly visits.

'And Dad resisted bitterly, of course. He was in poor health but refused to move house into somewhere smaller and more manageable, even though only Lizzie was still living at home and she was engaged and soon to be married. But after all the shouting matches we'd had, Dad and me, mainly over me going to church . . . we'd never been close and all that pushed us further apart . . . Well, in the end we said yes. We let the cottage. And spent the next five years in Asia.'

She flicked through the album again.

'Here, this is where we were mainly based, a high-rise apartment in Hong Kong which doubled as office and home. We also spent months at a time working out of a staff flat in Singapore when Peter had projects needing attention in Indonesia. Whenever the budget allowed I would travel with him and write up reports on various projects. Or I'd interview SaveAid workers travelling through Hong Kong or Singapore.'

'But wasn't it a bit overwhelming after the village here?'

'Remember – I'm really a city girl! No, I loved it. I took to Hong Kong from the minute I arrived. It was quite an experience. The flight arrived in the late afternoon and I'll never forget the taxi ride through the jam-packed streets of Kowloon and through the Crossharbour Tunnel to Hong Kong Island. Richard – he's SaveAid's Asia Pacific Director – was at the flat to meet us. I was exhausted after the flight. Well, we both were. But there was no way we could sleep. We roamed around the streets for hours, well after nightfall, fascinated by everything. The sights, the sounds, the smells of a city awake, restless and striving twenty-four hours a day – it was all wonderful to me. The England I left behind had little appeal right then. It was 1979, the time of those awful strikes. Remember?'

'Heavens, yes! Lorry-drivers, ambulance men, dustmen, sewerage workers – they were all at it, weren't they? All that garbage piled high in the streets.'

'Yes, it was a relief to get away from it, and the frenetic industry of Hong Kong was refreshing.'

'Well, a holiday in Portugal's the extent of my foreign travel.'

Helen picked up another album and began flicking through it.

'People always assume going to Hong Kong must have been a tremendous shock,' Alex continued.

'Funnily enough, I always think of it as being less of a dramatic transition than the change I made in becoming a Christian a couple of years earlier. Perhaps you can understand that. At my conversion I took on a whole new set of values. New values with all the repercussions on lifestyle. For years that was harder to adjust to than uprooting to Asia. When I got converted I had lots to learn about forgiveness, about honesty, about . . . oh, well, loads of things.

'But,' hesitating a little now, 'it was great that I didn't make any of those changes on my own.'

Neither Peter nor Alex realized just how significant it would be that they shared that evening of rebirth, that moment in time when a new Master was owned. The togetherness that was instinctive with them from the beginning was now anchored to what was arguably the ultimate in shared experience. A vague exposure to the Catholic Church had given Peter a head start on his new lifestyle in some ways — through he had perhaps more to unlearn than Alex did. He was always able to be more logical, more cerebral, about his new-found faith than she was.

'I'm sorry! Is that the time? I've kept you very late. I'm really sorry.'

'Don't be silly! I've had a wonderful afternoon. I've really enjoyed hearing about everything. It's just that Sarah usually rings around this time on Sundays and she's the sort to panic if she doesn't get an answer.'

Helen left Alex sitting, slightly bewildered, on the sitting-room floorboards, surrounded by photo albums. For a few hours Alex had been lost in the past and, surprisingly, been able to share it. Move vividly than ever the past seemed a place of security and warmth. And belonging.

Monday morning. There was a neat row of Hong Kong stamps on the blue envelope. Alex stooped down and lifted it from where it lay stark on the chipped terracotta tiles of the hallway. She opened it slowly, leaning for support on the wall.

It was a printed newsletter from Joyful Haven. Across

the top sheet Sister Bridget had scrawled in red biro, 'All missing you, Alex. No typhoons this summer! November promising to be lovely as ever. Write?'

Alex scanned the newsletter, suddenly breathless. Three new admissions in the last quarter. Two little brothers in regular foster care with a family at Clearwater Bay. An excursion to Lantau Island for swimming and a barbecue. Promise of a government grant for an extension for live-in staff. Donations update.

Nothing! Nothing! Nothing!

Until this minute she hadn't admitted to herself how much she wanted to get news of the child.

The rest of the morning she paced feverishly around the cottage, debating furiously with herself. Well, she had the clean break she wanted. Better, more logical, to build anew. But the little round face with brown eyes appeared, dreamy, and appealed silently. Resisting didn't seem important any more.

Finally, though the decision brought no peace, Alex rummaged in her suitcase in a corner of the bedroom till she found some notelets. She planned out a few sentences, several times crossing through and changing words, looking for a light touch, inventing a carefree, casual style. If Sister Bridget didn't believe the words, she would be sensitive enough to read between the lines, but Alex choked on total honesty. Still unsatisfied, she copied out the final draft in a more composed hand, and before she could have second thoughts she flung on her anorak, grabbed an umbrella and set out into the persistent rain towards the Post Office. She ran.

Joyful Haven. How vividly Alex could picture her first visit there. The name was spelt out on a faded wooden post jutting out of a cluster of bamboo trees grimy with dust. This was it. Alex slid the photocopied street map into her shoulder-bag and took out her notepad and pencil, together with a pack of tissues. She wiped her face and tied her hair back more firmly in its elasticated band. The ride through the back streets of Kowloon on the swaying PLB had left her grimy and sweating. It was a heavy overcast morning in August and temperatures as usual were already in the nineties.

Across the road, trade was brisk at the street market. A leather-skinned old man in a dirty singlet and baggy shorts was arranging a new delivery of ice blocks on his fresh-fish stall. Next to him, a woman juggled oranges and papayas into flimsy red plastic bags. A few late risers crouched over metal tables, shovelling their breakfast congee into their mouths and scanning newspapers.

Alex took in the old colonial building in front of her, wedged incongruously between two more modern blocks of tiny tenement flats. The front door was massive in gnarled wood and rusting hinges. The façade was crumbling grey stone, two storeys high, the uppermost favoured with a wide pillared verandah.

She rang the bell and heard it echo loudly inside, followed after some seconds by the slap of flip-flop rubber sandals on marble.

'You want?'

An old woman in the customary black pyjama suit peered up at her, and then led her across the hallway, empty save for a family of scrawny kittens tumbling over and around a cardboard box.

'Thank you, Auntie Yin. Would you get some tea for us, please?'

Sister Bridget introduced herself. She was a tall, stately-looking Canadian woman in her late forties, cool and slender in a plain navy cotton sleeveless tunic and trousers, and flat leather sandals. Her greying hair escaped in frizzy tendrils from a small white triangular headscarf tied at the back of her neck. Her face was pale and her eyes were a light blue-violet that was startlingly attractive.

'Alex Davis. From SaveAid. I think our director Richard called you about an article on the Home for the supporters' magazine?'

'Yes,' she admitted, soft-spoken, cautious. 'He did say you'd be coming this morning. But I'm not sure we can help. I mean, I'm not convinced we want this kind of publicity. Or any kind of publicity, in fact.' The violet eyes smiled.

Alex felt hot, dishevelled and flustered, and was glad that at this point in the conversation Auntie Yin appeared with a tray.

'Auntie! *Guhk fah chaah!* I'm sure our guest would prefer western tea!'

'No, no. *M gan yiu, sumsum. Ho jungyi yaam di guhk fah chaa,*' Alex protested.

Auntie Yin beamed at her toothlessly, laid the tray on the low table and backed out of the door. Surreptitiously, Alex slipped the notepad back into her bag.

Sister Bridget motioned her to sit.

'So, the young English reporter speaks Cantonese. And drinks chrysanthemum tea.'

Alex thought she detected a hint of humour in the voice.

'I'm taking a few language classes, but it doesn't amount to much more than a bit of basic survival. It's definitely not as easy as French and I was never brilliant at that! All those different tones!'

They sipped tea from the tiny rice-pattern cups and spoke of the typhoon forecast, and the front-page story in the *South China Daily News* about the abuse of Filipina maids. Alex glanced at her watch.

'And when did you first come to Hong Kong, Sister?'

'Ahh, a long time ago. So long ago, it's probably too late for me to think of leaving. Twenty-seven years. But you don't want to know about me. Surely you want to write about the children of Joyful Haven? In your article? Without the children, there's no story. Come on. That bell means it's morning break time. And since it's Saturday we have a full house. You must meet them. And, if I were you, I should get your notebook out.'

They exchanged conspiratorial smiles as they stood up.

Alex followed her up a flight of wooden stairs, and along a narrow corridor, with several glass-panelled doors opening left and right. She glimpsed four small dormitories, the walls painted in blue and green pastels, each containing six to eight metal framed beds or cots, all neat with matching cotton covers.

The dining-room was buzzing with noise. The banging of plastic beakers on tables. The scraping of metal chair legs across the tiled floor. The whirr of ceiling fans. And a symphony of lively chattering voices.

Twenty or more children aged from about three to nine or ten, mostly girls with identically severe-cut bobs of black hair with deep fringes, were sitting at low tables, drinking orange squash, demolishing biscuits and wedges of apple. All wore pale blue pinafores over T-shirts and shorts. Auntie Yin and two other black-pyjamaed amahs were keeping order and mopping up spills.

The far end of the room opened on to a wide balcony overlooking a garden, which must be a smaller copy of the balcony at the front of the building Alex had seen from the road. The tall wooden doors were tied back and she saw that the balcony was furnished with a large home-made playpen. Four or five younger tots rolled or crawled around inside, watched over by a westerner, a young woman with a friendly freckled face and short blonde hair. She was rocking a screeching furious-faced toddler on her hip.

Sister Bridget strode over to the balcony and Alex followed.

'Here, let me take her,' she said briskly, taking the child firmly in her arms.

'Hello,' volunteered the young woman, smiling broadly and offering her hand.

'Alex, let me introduce you to Sandie. She's from your part of the world, England, and has only been here a few months. SaveAid recruited her to do a year's placement with us. She's a student nurse taking time out of her studies to get some different experiences.

'And', looking down a little wearily at the child who had tired of shrieks and was now concentrating on shuddering, relentless sobs, 'Siu Ling is really giving Sandie a wealth of different experiences!'

'She's not always like this?' Alex asked.

'Most of the time, except when she's asleep!' answered Sandie, again with a wide smile.

'But we forgive her, don't we!' laughed Sister Bridget.

'Siu Ling's only been at Joyful Haven just over a week,' explained Sandie. 'And with her background we weren't expecting her to settle quickly. It'll take time. But here the speciality is love and patience. And we mustn't forget Sister's special medicine – prayer!'

'Is she typical of the kind of child that comes here?' Alex asked.

'No, she's not typical. She's very special. None of our

children are typical,' replied Sister Bridget vehemently, fixing Alex with those violet eyes.

Alex reddened under her gaze.

'I'm sorry, I didn't mean . . .'

Sister Bridget lowered her eyes.

'No, no, I was being unkind to you. That wasn't fair.'

The little girl was subsiding a little as Sister Bridget stroked her damp forehead.

'Siu Ling is mentally handicapped.'

'Oh, I didn't . . . I mean, I couldn't tell,' Alex said, confused.

'Actually, at first glance it is difficult to tell. She has Down's syndrome, and the trained eye could probably pick that up from the stubby fingers, the splayed toes, the set of her rather cute bullet-shaped head on her neck. At this age it's not very noticeable. But she's almost three, very small for her age and not walking yet.'

'Do you take in many handicapped children?'

The little girl twisted around, still sobbing, in Sister Bridget's arms and fixed her eyes on Alex.

'A few. They are more difficult to place with adoptive families, but we've had a number of successes, all with families overseas. Whereas the old superstitions and stigmas attached to handicap, especially mental handicap, die hard in this part of the world, western families are much more open to taking a special-needs child. And so we've been able to place several in loving homes in Canada, the US, England, and we've some interest from contacts in Australia and New Zealand.'

Siu Ling abruptly ceased her noise and made a lunge at Alex, twisting her fingers into the amber beads around her neck.

At the sound of a clanging bell the long dining-room

erupted into clamour and confusion as the children rose and were called out in small groups.

'I must go and get the older children started on their Saturday jobs. Perhaps I can leave you with Sandie for a while? She can answer most of your questions. Here, would you mind taking Siu Ling? She seems to have taken a liking to you, or at least to your beads.'

Without ceremony, she thrust the hot little body into Alex's arms and rushed off. Alex stared down into two suspicious brown eyes, deep wells of confusion and hurt.

EIGHT

'Lexa, love, any chance of getting that report on the women's hostel in Bangkok finished? Richard's chasing me for it. They faxed him about it from Oxford. Something about the print deadline being brought forward.'

Peter was flinging things into his briefcase ready for the monthly project update meeting and half day of prayer at Richard's flat.

Alex was ironing on the balcony.

'It's in the in-tray, but I haven't got to it yet,' she called out to him. 'Tell him I'll work on it over the weekend, and get it to him for first thing Monday.'

Peter put an arm round her waist from behind and nuzzled the top of her head.

'Look, I'll have to go. I'll be late. But can't you get it done today?'

'I'm out today. Don't forget the report on your trip to Bangladesh. I've printed it out. It's on top of the filing cabinet.'

'Got it already, thanks. What's on today, then? An

interview? Or the women's coffee morning? I really feel if it's the coffee morning you should give it a miss and get on with that Bangkok report. Richard was a bit tight-lipped about it, actually.' Peter crossed to the coffee table and snapped closed the briefcase.

'He'll have to wait.' Alex studied the shirt she was folding. 'I promised I'd lend a hand at Joyful Haven today.'

'Again? You spend more time there than at your desk these days.'

He gave a laugh, but Alex had already heard the edge in his voice.

'Sandie is taking her first day off for a month, and they need help with the little ones. Can you pick up a takeaway pizza for supper?'

'Can do. I must go. Bye, love.'

She hadn't meant to get so involved. But after the article on Joyful Haven was written and approved she found herself dropping in occasionally. Peter was, after all, so busy and sometimes away for weeks at a time travelling.

And when she was at the home it was hard to stand around while everyone was so busy, so she pitched in. She soon realized that Sister Bridget, despite her quick and sometimes acid tongue, was someone to admire. And Sandie, her bubbly youthfulness combined with genuine commitment, became a real friend. Alex enjoyed taking some of the pressure off them by turning up unexpectedly to help with the children. Sister Bridget would give her a grateful smile and dash off to the office to spend a few hours catching up with paperwork. At weekends there were outings to organize, homework to help with, reading out loud to listen to. On weekdays there was cleaning to do, clothes and sheets to be manhandled into the industrial-sized machines, always a pile of mending sitting

100

in the corner of the laundry – shorts and cotton tops and little blue pinafores. And always there were babies and toddlers to bathe, to change, to cuddle, to feed bottles or take for walks in the big rambling garden at the back of the house.

And then there was Siu Ling. Somehow it had become something of a personal challenge to help try to get through to this disturbed and angry little bundle. The child continued to stretch everyone's patience and understanding to the limits. She cried for indecipherable reasons, she scowled, she pouted.

'Here, Alex, read this. Then you'll understand some of the reasons why she's like she is.' Sandie thrust Siu Ling's case notes into her hands.

The baby girl had been born illegitimately to a fifteen-year-old. During the pregnancy there had been talk of grandmother raising the baby. But, born prematurely, she was weak and flaccid-limbed. And when it was obvious within a few hours of birth that Siu Ling was definitely mentally handicapped, the family felt they couldn't cope and signed her off into the care of the Hong Kong government. In addition to Down's syndrome, Siu Ling was born with a faulty heart valve and so was kept in hospital until she was strong enough for surgery. Afterwards, her recovery was slow, held up by several infections. By this time the child had become difficult and withdrawn, which the social worker largely attributed to her being deprived of warm physical contact in the early formative months of her life. There were also doubts about her hearing. Her fractious behaviour meant it was difficult to find an institution prepared to take her. Until Sister Bridget heard about her.

'We're trying a new tactic with Siu Ling this week,'

Sandie announced, as Alex handed back the file.

'You know how much she loves food! Well, Sister Bridget has decided we have to be a bit cruel to be kind. We're delaying her mealtimes while she's crying or throwing a tantrum, and offering her special titbits when she's quiet and more controlled.'

'Sounds like bribery and corruption to me,' Alex laughed. 'Is it working?'

'Certainly it seems to be having some effect,' grinned Sandie. 'I think she almost enjoyed being a bit calmer this morning to earn her breakfast porridge. And if I didn't know better, I might have thought she almost smiled when we finally started popping the spoon into her mouth!'

It was true. Siu Ling's outbursts of distress and rage began to lessen in intensity. Slowly, she was encouraged to start feeding herself. And soon she took her first few flat-footed steps. But progress was never consistent. For no apparent reason she would sometimes refuse to hold the spoon, or she would cling to the playpen bars and resist any coaxing to walk.

Feeling they were close to a breakthrough, Alex began to spend even more time with Siu Ling, playing building blocks with her on the floor, reading nursery rhymes in her quieter moments, leading her tottering and slow, holding her chubby hand, through the shady garden. The child often stared up at her long and hard, her unwavering gaze full of questions. Alex wondered if she was debating within herself whether to trust her. As yet, she didn't return anyone's smiles.

'I'm going to miss you. We're off to Singapore for two months soon. Will you miss me, I wonder?'

Siu Ling blinked, and her gaze drifted off into middle distance.

Joyful Haven, so full of life and activity, seemed a little world detached from the rest of Alex's life. Indeed, it was a place where she could temporarily forget what was happening outside. Because some of what was happening was painful.

Especially the discovery that the family she and Peter had assumed they would create together was unlikely ever to be.

This new bewildering pain was the first real assault on their still-young marriage.

'Talk to me! Talk to me! We have to share this together!' Peter begged her.

'Please, just leave me alone. Don't touch me. Go away. I'm not ready to share it. I have to work at it myself first, come to terms . . .' She lay face down on the bed, her body shaken by sobs.

'They might be wrong! We'll go to another doctor. Get a second opinion. We'll pray. You'll see. It'll be all right, Lexa. We'll pray. It'll be OK.' His voice tore from him, ragged, shocked, but as yet she couldn't handle his distress as well as her own.

'Leave me alone!'

Given time, they patched over the damage the doctor's report had inflicted. In Singapore they consulted a specialist but decided the frail chance of parenthood he held out to them was no fair exchange for the huge medical bills. Stumbling, they forced themselves to talk about childlessness, spelled out their shattered dreams to one another and wept in each other's arms. They did pray. But Alex insisted Peter tell no-one. God must be their only refuge and help.

Daily life, then, was subject to this new inner turmoil. At times Alex rose to heights of faith, believing that surely the God she loved would intervene in her failing body, plant her a baby to love. And alternately she fell to the blackest depths, tasting bitter shame and desolation, convinced of the unfruitfulness not just of her womb's relentless monthly cycle, but of her whole existence. Snapshots of babies and toddlers sent in bulging airmail envelopes from her three prolific younger sisters did nothing to soothe her.

Significantly, she lost interest in her writing and Peter became a reluctant go-between when she failed to meet deadlines for Richard.

'Look, you must let me tell him. If he knows, about us, about you, he'll understand. This . . . these things take a while to get used to. He'll understand why you're not coping. I can't keep making excuses!'

She grabbed his hand and pulled him down to the sofa.

'No! Don't go, yet. Please don't tell anyone! Especially not Richard. I'll sort myself out. I've already made a start on that piece about the new Philippines centre. I'll work on it tonight.'

Her voice was rising through a violent crescendo.

'Look, tell him I've got writers' block or something. Tell him I've got a cold. Tell him it's the time of the month, for goodness sake! That at least would have some truth in it. For me it's always going to be the time of the month, isn't it!'

The harshness of her own words stung her to tears.

Peter, frightened of the new violence uncovered in her, held her tight, waited, and whispered through her hair.

'I know this sounds selfish, love, but if you're not doing your work properly it sort of reflects on me. Can't you see that? We're a partnership. Just tell me if you've had enough and we can go back to England. I'll get another job. We've got the cottage. We can start again. Maybe after a while we can think about adopting. You know?'

After long minutes of silence, Alex sighed loudly. 'It's all right, Pete. It's me that's being selfish. I know how much you love this job. And I love my writing, too, when I can forget all this baby business. I will get over it. I will. Promise.'

She worked late on the Philippines article that night, knew it was far from her best, but had no heart to re-write it. She faxed it to England along with a fresh determination to tackle all the articles outstanding and make Peter really proud of her.

Partly as some peculiar form of penance, and partly because it was a mixed pleasure these days to see so many smiling children's faces, she limited herself to weekly visits to Joyful Haven from then on, and tried to concentrate more on her in-tray. And she took on the leadership of a women's Bible study group. The discipline of having to prepare for the weekly class was good for her and she felt her understanding of her own faith was growing in leaps and bounds as she taught the Bible in a structured way. She also took on some distance-learning units through a Bible school back in England and grappled with some basic Hebrew and Greek. She worked on the homework assignments late into the evenings when Peter was away.

One Friday morning Sister Bridget's face was particularly tense as she answered the door to her. Alex reflected how much she had come to respect and admire this woman, voluntarily childless, who had devoted her life to unwanted children.

'Trouble?' she queried.

'Nothing the Lord can't deal with!' Sister Bridget replied, her face brightening.

'Well, actually it's Siu Ling. She's been bothering us all week. She's going through one of her really stubborn phases. She's only really happy and settled when she's given one-on-one attention – and staff-wise we're stretched to the limits this weekend so there's no way we can give her the time she needs.'

Was it a sudden impulse? Or just the outward expression of something dormant in the recesses of her heart for months?

'Sister . . . could I . . .? I mean, how would you feel if I took her home with me for the weekend? I could give her some individual attention that might make all the difference. It's worth a try, isn't it? I'd be very careful with her.'

'Oh, I know, dear Alex! You'd take the very best care of her! But, these things are not best done on the spur of the moment. Stop and think it over first. Is Peter home this weekend? Perhaps you'd better call and speak to him. Wouldn't that be wise? You can use the phone in the office.'

There was a long pause on the end of the phone when she put her idea to Peter. He'd only visited the home once and Siu Ling's name was little more to him than one of the preoccupations that distracted his wife from more important matters.

'What'll we do with her all weekend? Won't we have to take her out, you know, do things with her?'

'I told you, just our time and attention will be everything to her. I'll bring a bag of toys and things from the home.'

'And where will she sleep?'

'Well, I don't know. Can't you be a bit more constructive instead of firing questions at me? We can use

106

that camping airbed thing, on the floor in our room.'

'I don't know, Lexa. My only really free weekend for months. I was looking forward to a quiet couple of days before the conference in Chiang Mai on Tuesday.'

'She'll be no bother. Honestly. I'll keep her out of your way when you're working. Do say yes, Peter!'

Another pause.

'OK! I can hardly say no, my love. You sound more enthusiastic than I've heard you for months.'

Strangely enough, from the start Peter was more relaxed with Siu Ling than Alex was. The responsibility weighed down on her rather too heavily. In her mind terrible and improbable scenarios played and replayed. Siu Ling drowning in the bath. Or climbing off the balcony. Or running under a bus. Or simply stopping breathing. She slept hardly at all those three nights, but lay hanging over the edge of the bed watching the child sprawled on the inflatable. Siu Ling, in contrast, slept deeply, breathing noisily.

And she was, for most of the time, unbelievably well-behaved.

'You didn't tell me what a sweet little pudding of a thing she is!'

Peter was enchanted by her, watching her struggle to pile up the plastic beakers Alex handed her. She pushed them over with the flat of her pudgy hand, her brow intense with concentration.

'We could take her over to the beach at Stanley for an hour tomorrow after church,' suggested Peter. 'What do you think?'

'Great! What about your report for Chiang Mai?'

'I'll try and get it done after she's in bed tonight, shall I?'

Siu Ling was hesitant about the beach. She took one look at the crowds and froze, her eyes wide with apprehension. Peter swung her into his arms and led the way. Siu Ling broke into a panting, wailing noise. Alex followed, crimson, sure that everyone was staring at them.

Finding a less densely populated spot wasn't easy, but they finally found a space where they could spread out their bamboo mats. Siu Ling, still wailing, gripped tightly on to Peter's arms and wouldn't let him lower her on to the mat. After several attempts, and with the decibel level rising, Alex suggested ice-creams would be a good diversion and ran off to get some. Thankfully, it worked.

'Why do you think she reacted like that?' Peter asked, half an hour later. Siu Ling, quiet now but very sticky, was digging her spade determinedly into the soft sand, but couldn't be persuaded to offload the contents into the bucket, preferring to pile the sand on the mat.

'I can't say. Probably she's not been to the beach before. Anything new seems a big ordeal to her till she gets used to it. That's just Siu Ling – rather unpredictable.'

They made one abortive trip down to the edge of the beach to try to wash the stickiness and sand off her, but the South China Sea was just one more new experience Siu Liung wasn't ready for. At the first loud wail, they retreated!

'It's been a really nice weekend,' Peter whispered that evening, as they lay in bed looking down at Siu Ling's flushed pink cheeks.

He stroked Alex's arm. 'I could quite get used to this ready-made family thing. What about you?'

'I don't know. I'm not really ready to think about it, Pete. Not yet. Do you mind?'

'OK. No hurry. But if you want Siu Ling to come and stay another weekend, that's fine with me.'

Sitting now in the cottage watching the creeping dusk, Alex fingered the new scar on her hand. Why had she sent the letter to Sister Bridget? The memories, so long suppressed, ran in rivers behind her eyes and could no longer be damned back. She felt again their horror, undiminished. 'Oh Jehovah Rapha,' she whispered. 'Where are you, the Lord who heals?'

Why had there been other weekends? If only she'd stopped it all there, halted everything after those first hesitantly happy few days. If only she could rewind the time, play back the hours and weeks and months a little, just a little, differently. How could something so good, so well-intentioned, lead to disaster? How could she know that by introducing this solemn-faced chubby little girl into their lives she was condemning herself to a life sentence of sorrow?

NINE

Some memories, of course, were indelible. As solid as walls.

The first wall that night had been the dense, warm human wall that formed itself brick by body in every standing and sitting space, along paved walkways, curved around hotel lobbies, banked along the traffic-cleared streets, on either side of the inky Victoria Harbour.

Picnickers, proprietorial and loud from staking claim to prime sites since early afternoon, sprawled in family groups over the pavements outside City Hall. Polystyrene rice boxes spilled half-finished into the grey foam licking the harbourside; abandoned McDonald's wrappers and Yeo's cartons dribbling sugar cane and lychee juice collected in flotillas around bins and bollards. Baby-faced policemen straddled motor bikes, clutched walkie-talkies, perspiring shiny under the street lamps. The city's most exhaustive crowd control exercise of the year was under way and each man knew where he was pegged on the operations map. The bigger-and-better-every-year multi-million-dollar Chinese New Year fireworks display was soon to begin. The

Year of the Rat was being heralded in style on a clear February evening in Hong Kong. The barges from which the cascades of rocketing colour would be launched were poised, bobbing shadows in position on the water.

Hundreds, thousands more people poured in streams from the regular three-minute dockings of the Star Ferry fleet. The flow checked, observed the black density of heads blocking Edinburgh Place and deflected, largely right, seeking vantage-points in the concrete nesting-areas of the General Post Office or Exchange Square, or along the exposed outcroppings of the finger piers for vehicle ferries. Filipina maids, gleefully free for a few hours, as interested in seeking out their friends as in watching the fireworks extravaganza, chattering shrilly in Tagalog, headed in hand-holding gangs for rendezvous points inland, in Statue Square, in Chater Garden, or in the marbled entrance-ways of department stores in Des Voeux Road. Brazen shop windows everywhere glowed with red and gold streamers, sprays of peach blossom and miniature kumquat trees hung with perfect orange fruit.

And still they came, building the wall. Disgorged from the tiled Mass Transit Railway exits at Admiralty Centre, swelling bands went to meet up with those they knew who worked in offices on high floors at the Bank of America Building or Jardine House. All glass-fronted offices with harbour views were worth their weight in gold tonight. And then there were those envied ones whose far-sighted monied acquaintances had long ago booked rooms for the evening, at a premium, in hotels with the coveted angles to the murky waterway, especially the Furama with the revolving restaurant, the Mandarin Oriental and the Hilton; or, on the other side of the brief black water, the pink-bricked New World.

Expatriates and upwardly mobile locals living on the Peak prepared to receive guests for cocktails, magnanimous in sharing their section of the view from dozens of well-tended balconies. Down below, in Lan Kwai Fong, in nightclubs and bistros buried in Wyndham and D'Aguilar Streets, barmen checked stocks and watches, flicked channels, from Jade to Pearl, wondering which broadcast of the display to favour.

'Peter, are you still in the shower?' Alex yelled from the lounge. 'We need to be going.'

Thrusting a hairbrush into Siu Ling's hand to distract her, Alex swept her on to her back on the sofa before she could protest, and changed the disposable in record time. She checked the batteries in her hearing aids and then dressed the little six-year-old in dark green corduroy trousers and a warm sweater, while the child concentrated on making unsuccessful lunges at her hair with the brush.

'Pete gumin?' she queried, arching her eyebrows.

'Pete coming,' Alex agreed. 'Look, you should be doing up these shoes yourself, but there's no time.'

'One, do, one, do,' she intoned.

'Oh, yes, I haven't forgotten. One, two, buckle my shoe, three, four . . .'

'Free, four, free, four . . .'

'Ready?' Peter appeared in the doorway, his jacket over his arm. He was grinning and held up a bunch of jingling keys.

'Richard said we could use the van tonight. New Year in style!'

'Great! Except – I'm not sure it's really an advantage. The crowds will be so thick. And don't they close the main roads to traffic down by the harbour?'

Alex struggled to get Siu Ling's arms into her anorak.

She wouldn't let go of the hairbrush, and was rocking from side to side, stamping her feet and shouting, 'One, do, one do, free, four.'

Peter grabbed her and lifted her up, squeezing her to his chest.

'Hey, little Miss Tubby, she grew so-o-o-o chubby.'

Siu Ling shrieked and wriggled.

'No, Nunky Pete! Pete tubby! Pete tubby. Bad boy.'

'Pete, don't get her too excited!'

'OK. I'll take her down while you get your coat and lock up. Oh, and bring a couple of cushions to put in the back. Come on, Miss Tubby.'

Alex collected raincoat, bag and cushions and crossed to the windows to close the curtains. For a few seconds she stood there, watching the two emerge eight floors below, her long-striding husband adjusting his step to the little girl's shuffling, short-stepping, flat-footed amble. As Alex gazed down, Siu Ling lifted her face to him. Though Alex couldn't see her features, she felt sure she was wearing that glazed look of distant and impenetrable lostness that tested understanding. At the best of times, it was a look that challenged them. At the worst of times, it was a look that alienated them. It was, though, a look they already loved well. Siu Ling had been spending weekends with them irregularly now for almost three years. Alex often reflected on the fact that they were all three motherless. Was it significant? Did they belong together?

Inevitably, they were assembling an album of memories that involved the three of them. In the early days they made lots of mistakes, choosing outings and activities that proved disappointing because too sophisticated and demanding. Now they'd learned that the simple pleasures communicated best to her.

Siu Ling would never tire of trips on the MTR when she was allowed to put her own ticket though the machine at the station barrier. The destination in itself was not important. The whoosh of air as a train arrived at the underground station made her jump up and down with anticipation.

Then there were excursions to eat out. Siu Ling had a phenomenal appetite, although she grew hardly at all. A walk would be tackled with great energy with the promise of a visit to Dunkin' Doughnuts at the end. McDonald's and Burger King were also favourites, although the menu could never be varied. Cheeseburger and french fries, with plenty of ketchup, and hot apple pie in its red cardboard envelope. Any suggestion of a different menu choice might trigger a major sulk, or even a tantrum.

A walk in the zoo garden with a long time to study the flamingoes was another high scorer. Reading her favourite Ladybird story of 'The Enormous Turnip' never failed to produce giggles. Shopping for new shoes absorbed her, but the shoes invariably had to be red. Given the security of oft-repeated outings and growing accustomed to their flat and the playground around the corner, Siu Ling became more relaxed, learned to say a few words. She trusted them, appeared happy to be with them. But Alex was devastated that she didn't ask for them or seem to miss them at all when they were away for weeks at a time.

Peter was able to be more philosophical about it. 'You don't *know* she doesn't miss us,' he insisted. 'She doesn't use the same signals as we do, that's all.'

For several weeks they had seen little of her. Peter had been visiting project staff in Thailand and Alex had been tied to her desk working on a new brochure for fund-raising. That afternoon they had collected her for an outing to the New Year fireworks display.

'Richard told me about a place we can park near Pottinger Street. It's not so far to walk from there,' Peter said when she arrived at the van.

He added, with mock theatricality, 'Afterwards, when all five and a half million of Hong Kong's citizens are struggling down into the deep dank bowels of the MTR, we'll be strolling back to the luxury of the SaveAid van . . .'

'Some luxury!' Alex interrupted, unaccountably irritated. She passed over the cushions.

She got into the van and strapped herself in, then stretched her arm back over the car seat, locating Siu Ling in a sitting position on the cushions. Fortunately, Siu Ling was in cooperative mood, sliding her fingers pensively up and down the zip of her red anorak and making one of her clucking comfort noises.

Peter's good mood was not to be spoilt.

'. . . And then we can whisk this little dumpling back to Sister Bridget in no time. We might even get an early night? Whoops! Sorry, Lexa, thought that was the gear lever, honest!' He squeezed her knee and then, grinning widely, turned the key in the ignition.

In spite of having no friends in literally high places, and arriving at the harbourside fairly late, they were soon surprisingly well-positioned for a good view of the fireworks. The crowds, good natured, made way, pushing them forward, encouraging them to move here or there into a better spot. Even Alex's natural pessimism was dispelled.

Now Siu Ling perched on Peter's shoulders, clutching too tightly round his neck, staring open-mouthed and drooling, occasionally letting out staccato shrieks of delight as the extravagance of rainbow stars burst overhead.

They found themselves jostling against an old Chinese

116

amah who filled Siu Ling's hand with longgan and walnut chews and tucked a red laissee packet into her anorak pocket, despite their protests.

'*Kung Hei Fat Choy*,' Alex greeted her. 'Happy New Year!' The old woman gave a chuckle. Siu Ling was already sucking the rice paper off the first sweet, but Alex managed to divert the rest into her bag.

As the last echo of sky-high explosions died away and the heavens returned to empty blackness, as the last chorused 'waaahs' floated into the smoky ether, the wall began to melt from the edges. Some were heading for tables reserved for family banquet celebrations in the hotels and restaurants, others streaming towards the underground. Alex and Peter found their way to a wall near the ferry terminus to wait for the crowds to thin.

Siu Ling sat between them, eyes drooping, mouth and cheeks stained. Peter looked at Alex over the child's thick mop of black hair.

'Have you . . . have you thought any more, you know, about what we discussed when I phoned from Bangkok last week?'

He took her hand. She said nothing and after a few minutes he continued.

'Of course you have. I've been thinking and praying about little else since we finally had the courage to talk it through. And if I know you, you've thought of little else, either, have you?'

They stared out over the water. The ferry service re-entered its domain and was getting into the swing of its ceaseless service to and fro between Hong Kong Island and Kowloon. The first of the green and white ships pulled away, both decks crammed with people. Alex narrowed her eyes till she could make out the name, *Twinkling Star.*

She had decided about her own love for the child, but hesitated to believe it was for ever. And the fact that there was so little return to their love bothered her, sometimes even made her angry. Not just angry with the child, but angry at herself for her inability to love without condition. So, though they'd talked at last and at length about adoption, Alex was unresolved. And she was anxious about Peter's love. She needed to know if he could love Siu Ling for herself.

If he loved her only for my sake, because he felt I needed a child, Alex was thinking, that wouldn't be enough. Not fair on her.

Yet there was a sense in which she felt it unreasonable to question his love, so held back from voicing her fears, knowing that, if anything, Peter had always been more accepting of Siu Ling and her differences than she was. She swallowed the lump in her throat, but was unable to speak.

Peter broke the silence again.

'Well, it's a huge responsibility. Frightening. But we've talked it through as far as we can and I think we both know what's involved. Or at least we know as much as we can know right now. It would mean huge changes in our life.'

His tone was slow, measured. Alex knew that he'd been waiting for her to bring up the subject for days, and had the speech already prepared, memorized. She couldn't help smiling.

His assured voice faltered a little.

'Well, I think we could start asking a few questions at Joyful Haven. If we could get the paperwork started before we go on leave . . .'

'But . . .' Alex hesitated for the longest time. 'Do we love her? Love her enough? To cope with all her problems?'

118

'Honestly, I don't know. Maybe not yet, not enough. But, I think maybe we will. In time.'

He looked down. Siu Ling was sleeping against his arm, breathing regularly, mouth open. He pushed her fringe from her eyes.

'Look at her! Like this, you could almost think there was nothing . . . She looks just like a little angel when she's asleep.'

You could almost think there was nothing wrong with her. That's what he'd been about to say. Could they love her enough not to mind about her disabilities? The dependence which gave her a certain appeal as a helpless little child might make her a pressing and ugly burden as a young adult. Alex peered into the future but saw nothing.

Peter lifted the sleeping child into his arms, cradling her head against his neck.

'We could mention it to Sister Bridget tonight, if you like. Ask her to get the wheels in motion. I rather think she's been waiting for us to broach the subject.'

And still Alex said nothing.

They began to weave away from the waterside. The narrow steep streets were still packed with crowds parading New Year clothes, determined to enjoy the biggest holiday of the year. Little girls in flounced skirts and their brothers in bow ties and braces darted in circles, waving coloured torches and light sticks. Conversation in brash guttural Cantonese, unashamedly loud, was flung in staccato exchanges from one side of the street to the other, punctuated by uninhibited laughter. Impromptu stalls were balanced on bicycles or set up on trays on the pavements, and offered chrysanthemum tea, iced Seven Up, gift-wrapped dried mushrooms and battery-operated somersaulting puppy dogs.

As Peter tried to lay her on the cushions in the back of the van, Siu Ling woke, whimpering.

'Maybe if I take her on my lap, she'll drop off again,' Alex suggested.

But all the soothing sounds Alex could summon from her non-maternal repertoire failed to calm her. Though Alex cradled her and rocked her on her lap, she began to cry with growing deliberation. Alex's mind raced through possible causes. A bad dream? A pain somewhere? As they turned out of Pottinger Street, nosing through the crowds and then drawing away from the people downhill, the child wriggled and squirmed on Alex's knees. She screwed up her face, squeezing fat tear drops out of her eyes. Her wet mouth widened as she forced out persistent panting shrieks, rising in volume.

'Lexa, can't you stop her! Keep her quiet. That noise . . .'

Suddenly a rush of anger and panic swamped Alex.

'I'm doing my best! She's not a machine! Perhaps she's not well. I . . . I can't . . . I don't know how to! She's . . . it's not easy to understand why she . . . Don't you see, it's always going to be this hard, to be her mother, trying to understand her, trying to get through the barriers. Oh, God, it's no good, Peter! I'm not going to be able to cope, we're not going to be able . . . I do love her, but . . .'

It was within seconds of this, Alex's frustrated outburst, that the next wall loomed ahead, a movie-still framed by the windscreen, frozen for ever in the mind, the memory, the heart. Alex saw it intensely, minutely noted its firm greyness, its rough, flaking surface and paler grouting. The brief prelude to the wall was just a flashing blur of offstage activity. One second her arms were around the struggling child, restraining, but the next Siu Ling broke free and there was a sprawl of arms and legs, a jerking to the right which ricocheted to the left. There was a nightmare symphony of discords – Siu Ling's crazed shriek, Alex's low despairing moan, the whine of whirring metallic revolution, the crackling folding of collision. And her love's astonished, sighing intake of air.

Though low, she heard it. Peter's last breath.

How long did she sit staring at the grey wall? She was overtaken by an unearthly dreaming, a kind of frozen muteness that blanketed her from real touching, real hearing, real seeing. She wanted to go home. She wondered if she'd brought her stored-value underground ticket with her but her hand wouldn't reach to her pocket. Siu Ling's whimpers came from somewhere near her feet.

Much later, waking but not awake in the chill whiteness of some alien world, Alex still saw the wall. Her eyes ran over its crevices, fabricating its cobwebs and mossy shadows endlessly, exploring the crumbling exterior, trying to divine the impregnable interior.

People came and made soft sounds that didn't reach her ears. Some wept. Some prayed. She saw and felt nothing but the grey wall. After some time its familiarity was strangely comforting, though never warm. From picturing it in front of her, she extended it, stone by grey stone, till it reached around her and behind her, above her and below her. She built it closer.

The distancing numbness stayed with her and within her stone fortress as the days passed, each one a slow eternity. Bouquets of flowers wilted and were removed. Grapes wrinkled. Cards buckled and bowed and were tucked into the locker drawer. Starched sheets assumed a strange homeliness. She slept and slept, dreamless and drugged, her back to the door, face to another wall, smooth and blank, antiseptic pale green. There were whispers she cared not enough to decipher, ghostly faces she cared not enough to identify. Except that Sister Bridget came, and sat silently, tears on her cheeks. Once, just once, they brought the child in, and she stood with a question in her brown eyes and a half-smile of recognition on her little round red lips, but Alex turned away in terror to weep and sleep once more. Days were measured by the slight but regular spaces between the pills brought in plastic cups, and confirmed by the alternating sunlight and street lamplight filtered through woven bamboo blinds.

At long last there came an April morning when the sensations to her skin felt real and firm. Alex stroked the thin cotton bedcover with her fingers and felt the warmth her own body generated. That day the nurse had features. Alex observed her glossy hair and shy eyes, appreciated the strength of her slim arms as she helped her sit. The green tea was bitter, the congee salty. It tasted good. It was the first day of the rest of her life. It was the day she knew she wanted to live again, but barely. She set her face to an uphill road.

TEN

Free falling during the time in hospital, Alex wondered if the safety net existed. Her wondering was passive, since passion had fled, locked behind the wall. But the wondering was never idle. With curious detachment, she considered the saving power of her salvation. For years she claimed the distinction of living in God's favour, while acknowledging no merit on her part. The snuffing out of the light that was Peter made her question who she would be when finally she came down to the ground.

A kind of numb somnambulism was cotton wool to her hurts for the first months after the accident. Returning pain heralded guilty reality – that within her was still some vestige of appetite for life. Her leg itched ferociously inside the plaster, like the questions inside her head. She scanned her body for bruises and other evidence of spilt blood, but found the marks were healing with an enthusiasm that mocked her distress.

She felt old overnight and abandoned. The past had never seemed more wonderful, the problems of those days faded into insignificance. She had not appreciated the daily blessings she had enjoyed, had not been thankful enough for the gift of her husband, her lover, her friend. The distress of Job haunted her: *'Oh, that I were as in months past, as in the days when God watched over me; when his lamp shone upon my head, and when by his light I walked through darkness; just as I was in the days of my prime, when the friendly counsel of God was over my tent; when the Almighty was yet with me.'* She wept again and again over the escape she had missed, for to have fled heavenwards with him from the mangled wreckage would have seemed just, as well as joyful.

Since escape was her lot, she knew she should work towards receiving it as a gift. But what a task that would be.

Her frame, despite the absence of lasting scars, looked shrunken, hollow and stooping, altering in painful parallel to the inner self. She was horrified at the staring, dark-eyed ghost in the mirror. A physiotherapist was sent, but Alex's commitment to the exercises was at best wavering.

Finally, though, it was time to leave the green-white cocoon of the hospital, and she insisted that she would return to the apartment, and return alone.

There was a mountain of mail in the hallway letterbox. Up eight floors, she unlocked the security grille and let herself into the apartment. The curtains were closed, though being of some light gauzy cloth, the acid-bright sun filtered through to pattern the polished wooden floor. The humid air was heavy, choking, and she unlatched and drew back the full-length sliding glass doors that opened on to the balcony.

She rifled through the post. Several circulars offering Peter computer software bargains. One or two of those cards she'd come to dread, embossed, pastel-hued, featuring lilies. A postcard from Sandie, on honeymoon in Cyprus. Since leaving Hong Kong after her year's placement, she'd been nursing at a large Edinburgh hospital where she'd met a certain desirable young Scottish obstetrician. She still kept in touch.

The phone rang. Alex jumped.

'Missee Davis? Wah Loong Tailor, missee. Many weeks we try phone you. We deliver curtains today? Ready long, long time.'

She whispered back.

Then, slowly, she made a pilgrimage, touching with fingertips the everyday trivia that had been abruptly dispossessed: the running shoes abandoned by the front door, the razor blades on the bathroom shelf, a shirt sleeve hanging over the edge of the linen basket, the guitar propped against the sofa. Clues, all significant, all with their own stories to tell. Such fables were set in the past, starting, 'Once upon a time'. She left them all where they were. For a while they would speak to her, and only when all that could be said was said, would they be discounted and removed.

She searched the past for memorials to set up. Wasn't there some romantic tune they claimed as their own that she could play, and replay, indulging in its sentiment? Some poem, some flower, some shrine to their together-ness? Nothing came to mind. Such ordinary extraordinary love.

Her return to the apartment marked the onset of the nightmares. Night after night the grey wall reared up, monstrously proportioned, centre stage. In the wings flitted snippets of colour, most vividly the red of an anorak and the red of escaping life. There were echoed and slightly varying renditions of the script. No prompter needed.

Sometimes the wall was curiously juxtaposed with a city-centre scene revisiting her with the ricochet of thunder and the screech of brakes. Sometimes she glimpsed below the wall the yellow Avon foam.

At first she fought the nightly apparitions, battled to suppress them. Then, with a philosophical submission new to her, she accepted them, let them replay. She woke sweating and shaking, wide-eyed, and wandered the darkened rooms. She made tea and lay on the sofa, longing for the dawn. She reached for her Bible, her Hebrew commentary and notebook. She began a study, to distract and comfort, on the character-revealing names of the God who now seemed silent and perhaps gone away. Sometimes she prayed, determined but not fervent, to know him in all such wonderful ways as his names described. Jehovah Rapha: the Lord who heals. El Shaddai: the all-sufficient One. El Roi: the God who sees. Jehovah Shalom: the Lord is peace.

And Jehovah Shammah: the Lord who is there.

Her head accepted but her heart was resentful and cold.

Messages from England beckoned 'Come', but she was not ready to leave Hong Kong. Here the fragments of a shared life, though far from remarkable, were still warm. She made pilgrimages, to the shady park behind the apartment where they'd listened to cicadas at dusk, the shopping mall where they'd bought a silk tie to send for Uncle Tom's birthday, the tram stop where they'd got drenched in a sudden downpour and the heel had come off her shoe. His body was consigned to ashes with all due ceremony, but his spirit met her everywhere. Such meetings were as sweet as plums, and she was not ready to say goodbye.

After a few drifting days, she asked to resume working

for SaveAid. Just temporarily, she said, until she decided what to do. Richard, frowning and anxious but overworked, agreed. Resuming other social contacts seemed impossible. She felt angry when people were awkward and embarrassed when they bumped into her, though she knew she was unreasonable. Working on administration details for Richard, she felt safe and useful. She opened and answered mail, banked donations, worked on the next newsletter, protected behind her own efficiency.

Sister Bridget phoned, but Alex answered her like a stranger and allowed no space for discussion. One day she was invited by three friends for coffee at one of her favourite haunts – the rooftop tea-shop at the YMCA in Salisbury Road, with its stupendous view of the harbour. Alex accepted, but when she was with them she found her attention wandered. Their conversation sounded to her like the babble of schoolgirls. 'You can't possibly know yet what life is all about, so I must excuse you all while resenting your innocence,' decided Alex, primly sugaring her coffee and then remembering it was three years since she'd taken sugar in coffee. Later, she wept for her cold and judging heart that was alienating people at the very time she needed them most.

Reluctantly, she started to box up Peter's books and clothes, the minutiae of daily life now redundant and gathering dust. He would want his things to be used. It was the half-finished, never-to-be-completed items that hurt most. There was the badminton racquet he had left on top of the wardrobe, intending to take it to be re-strung. The shirt with a missing button, tucked into the mending pile behind the ironing-board. The biography in the bedside cabinet he'd not finished reading, the page marked with a ticket from a bus ride to Stanley Market.

And then there was the advance booking for two flights back to England for eight months' leave. Alex finally got around to phoning the travel agent, cancelling one and asking her indulgence while she considered the other.

A life undone. Therefore things to be undone. If only they had been less well organized. Plans made would for ever be unfulfilled. They had been looking forward to the eight months' leave they'd earned by their five-year contract in Asia. Four months would have been entirely theirs, followed by four months for deputation and fund-raising meetings for SaveAid before their return.

Sorting and tidying outwardly, inwardly Alex was in chaotic disarray. The future was a blank page she hesitated to mark. One stifling June evening she got around to snipping the pink nylon string from the parcels of curtains that had been delivered. The honeymoon cottage in an Oxfordshire village seemed a distant dream. She and Peter had made ambitious, somewhat fanciful plans for renovating it that summer. They had let it out initially, but when the first tenancy finished they'd not bothered to re-let, and had wanted to make good the neglect of several years.

She checked the measurements of the flowing lengths of cotton, bronze flowers and jade leaves swirling on a rich cream background. Suddenly, the bright colours were an offence to her, and she bundled them back into the brown-paper wrappings.

And then, months later, here were the curtains again, to be delivered the second time.

'Mrs Davis? Sharon, of Good Fortune Freight, London office, here. Your crates have been cleared at the port. Can we deliver to you in Oxfordshire tomorrow?'

The brown-paper parcels lay on the top of the first crate.

Alex recalled the haste with which she had re-tied the string to remove the yards and yards of the stuff from sight. She re-opened them hurriedly, keen to make the curtains the crowning glory to her newly decorated sitting-room. She congratulated herself on the complementing closeness of jade leaf to jade door, cream cotton to cream walls. A good match. Like them.

Now she stood in the sitting-room staring out at the first frost on the fence, fingering the bright cotton stuff hanging lifeless, on which she fancied still lingered a musty foreign scent. She wondered at the strange paralysis preventing her from continuing the renovation, begun so energetically two months ago. She had unpacked less than half the freight boxes heaped in the hall. Everywhere she looked she stumbled and tripped over the past and it held her up, pinned her down, kept her transfixed, walled her in.

The next morning, when the postman again passed her by and the cottage seemed full of echoes, she jumped into the car and drove like an escaped criminal to Swindon. She was thinking too much of herself and needed to focus elsewhere.

She parked with difficulty. The pedestrian shopping precinct was wild with shoppers, some bustling, some drifting blank-eyed with the tide. The first store, hot and airless, jangled with piped music, an assault of plastic seasonal brightness. Tinselled lanterns and cardboard cut-out Santas and reindeer larger than life swung from the ceilings. Each till had a long snake of clucking, sighing customers, shifting their feet, weighed down with over-flowing wire baskets.

Alex retreated to the quieter backwaters of an old-fashioned department store that still had counters and polished wood floors, and finally tracked down what she was looking for in the motoring accessories section. She studied the different plaids on offer in the heap of folded travelling rugs and chose something subdued in dark green and maroon. She shook her head and grinned. No doubt he would find something to complain about it. She would drive over to the Grange tomorrow and deliver it. She rehearsed how she would be caring, thoughtful, talk gaily of Christmas. Perhaps even suggest an outing. Why was she always offering the olive branch, yet always felt he was the chief offender in their jagged relationship? Never mind. She would do it. Bury the past. Force herself to play the part and she might come to believe in it herself. Whatever else, inescapably, he belonged to her and she to him.

She remembered how she struggled years before with thinking of God as her Father. Heavenly Father. Holy Father. The words themselves had at first a hollow ring to them. Fatherhood was tied up with fear and hunger and unreliability. Those negative images had inhibited her for weeks as she wrestled with understanding what God was like. But God was not modelled on her father, as Jackie had explained. Human fathers, and mothers too, were modelled on God, but imperfectly so.

After paying for the rug, Alex made for the children's book department. She selected a collection of nursery rhymes with thick card pages. She bought wrapping paper and ribbon. After a cursory trip to Tesco, she was on her way back to the cottage, feeling more pleased and positive than for weeks.

On her way home she stopped at the garage in the village. As she parked outside the repair workshop, a man in his mid-fifties made his way towards her, briskly rubbing his hands on a bundle of rags.

'Can I help, miss?'

'I hope so. The car's being a bit fussy starting. I've only had it a matter of weeks. My brother-in-law arranged it all for me. I'm afraid I'm a bit of an amateur as far as mechanics goes.'

Whistling, he started the engine and lifted the bonnet. After a few minutes, he announced the result of his examination.

'Starter motor's fine. Needs a new battery, I'm afraid.' His tone was apologetic. 'It's the time of the year, you know. First few frosty mornings and it's a bit too much if your battery's getting on a bit. And this one looks like it's giving up the ghost.'

Alex looked undecided.

'You just driving through?' he asked, taking off his cap and scratching his head.

'No. I live here. But I've been away quite a while.' She described her cottage.

'That pretty place on the back road? Come to think of it, perhaps my daughter-in-law's mentioned you to me. Mandy Evans?'

'Oh, yes!'

'Now, don't you go worrying that Douglas Evans is the sort to take advantage of women drivers who don't know much about cars. In a small place like this nearly all my trade comes because of having a good reputation. I can't afford *not* to be honest if you know what I mean!'

She returned his smile. 'Well, if you're certain it's the battery . . .'

'Don't have a new one in stock, I'm afraid. But I can order one and it shouldn't take more than a couple of days. Shall I go ahead?'

'Yes, please. And thank you.'

They shook hands rather solemnly and Alex scribbled him a note of her telephone number.

Driving away from the garage and through the village, Alex spotted Mandy herself, complete with toddler in pushchair and four-year-old in tow. Mandy began to wave at her vigorously, so Alex slowed and brought the Metro to a halt at the kerb.

'Alex! I tried to call you earlier.' Mandy smiled nervously. She looked tired and red-eyed.

'Thing is, I'm a bit desperate to get a babysitter for around six o'clock tonight. Just an hour probably, hour and a half maximum. Something urgent's cropped up and no-one seems free to help. Shaun's gone to pick up a breakdown and won't be back till late. I don't suppose you could help, could you? Bit of a cheek asking you, I know. I'd be ever so grateful.'

Alex swallowed hard, focusing on the little boy hopping up and down on his red-booted feet. She hesitated, looked up and watched the doubt creep over Mandy's face.

'I'm sorry. I can't . . . It's not really . . . No, I'm sorry. I'm not free this evening. I'm not actually very good with children. I'm sure you'll be able to find someone else, someone better. Sorry.'

Alex wound up the window and drove off before Mandy could reply.

As she arrived, joyless now, at the front door, chilled by the keen wind and weighed down with bags of shopping, Alex could hear the phone ringing. She thrust the bags into the porch and felt for the keys in her pocket. She reached the phone as it stopped ringing. She waited for the caller to try again, but there was silence. Like so many small things, it unnerved her disproportionately.

She made a cup of tea, switched on the radio and took

out a packet of mince pies. First of the season. By tradition, so Mum always told them as kids, a wish could be made. I wish . . . I wish . . .

The phone rang again.

'Mrs Davis? Sister Ellen Hendry here. From Cairnhill Grange. I'm sorry to have to give you some rather bad news about your father . . .'

She was efficient. Gave all the necessary details with all the necessary concern. And Alex answered with controlled detachment. It was only when she put the phone down that the pounding dam exploded in her head.

'It could have happened any time.' Those were her words. If at any time, why now? Why now when she was arming herself with forgiveness and bracing herself to reach out?

Grief was doubled. Not for what had existed between them, since it was measured as a mere ghost of a relationship. A muddied, insubstantial connection, illumined by the occasional fleeting understanding. But there was sorrow for what had been missed, what might have been, what they'd neither of them ever attempted to explore or create. More evidence of unfruitfulness. Along with the tears flowed anger and guilt, and the tears fed on past hurts and effected no healing.

'Can't wait to get away from yer old Dad, can yer!'

She remembered the accusations spat out with venom, cloaking any softer feelings at the farewell.

'Miss high and mighty! All this caring about other people half way round the globe, niggers and chinkies and all they damn foreigners the likes of me fought against in the war. Who's gonna lend a helping hand to yer own flesh and blood then? After all I bin through, strugglin' to bring you up decent after yer Mum walked out on the whole lot of us? Carry on! See if I care a bloody thruppeny bit if I never sees you again!'

And, hardening her heart, she didn't care enough to try any more to explain, dismissing his prejudice with something that looked like disdain.

She'd sent postcards, dozens of them over the years, to which he never once replied. But when he'd had the heart attack two years ago and she'd rushed home and then, emergency over, helped with moving him into the Grange, she'd found all the postcards, well-thumbed, kept in a biscuit tin on the sideboard. And Lizzie told her how he used to show them to all the neighbours, boasting about his travelling daughter to the point of boredom.

ELEVEN

All these years on, and the house in Stonebridge Road was still cold. Lizzie and Terry seemed not to notice.

'We'll probably get around to putting in central heating next year,' said Lizzie vaguely. 'But we thought it was more urgent to get the kitchen sorted out.'

She waved her hand at the cream and brown units and built-in hob. The tiny scullery, coal-shed and storage room had been combined to effect a good-sized kitchen, though rather dark. They'd also, Alex noticed with a smile, replaced the front door with something in fake oak and dimpled glass that made her think of galleons and pirates.

Lizzie, or 'young Lizzie' as she was always known in the family, was the youngest of the four daughters and most reminded Alex of the mousy misunderstood mother who'd walked out of their lives and eventually, some months of wandering later, into the Avon. Lizzie, who'd been seven when they'd been so dramatically bereft, always insisted she couldn't remember anything about her namesake. Alex's memories were also strangely misty. She remembered a pair of small rough hands rhythmically wringing out woollens at the deep sink in the scullery. Wisps of black hair escaping from a Paisley headscarf. Dark brown deep-set eyes that had no pattern anywhere. All four girls had the pale blue Travers eyes and brown hair.

Stonebridge Road belonged to Lizzie and Terry now. When they'd got married, Terry had been unemployed and had simply moved in, and when Dad had been moved out to the Grange they applied to the Council to buy the house. Today they played the part of hosts to the funeral gathering.

'It's a shame Anne couldn't get here,' said Lizzie, handing round a plate of sausage rolls, a baby on her hip. 'Did everyone read her card on the mantelpiece? And seen the latest picture of the boys?'

'Reading between the lines, she's got more interesting things to do than come to her Dad's funeral,' added Terry, with a snigger.

Mary drew deeply on her cigarette, and pursed her lips.

'It's no good jumping to conclusions,' she said.

'She's a bit of a dark horse, if you ask me,' announced Terry, determinedly raising his voice. 'Gets every penny she can out of Dave in the divorce settlement, not to mention this wonderful dream house they're supposed to have in Melbourne, he takes custody of the kids, and then within weeks she's writing from a different address hinting that there's a new man in her life!'

'As I said, it's no use jumping to conclusions,' said Mary sharply. 'And I think we'd all appreciate it if you didn't talk like that when the children are around. I'm sure Anne would have been here if she could manage it. Don't you think so, Adrian?' She inclined her head to her husband, who was sprawled on the sofa with a sherry in his hand.

136

'I expect that's the case,' Adrian contributed in his pompous tones, fingering the buttons of his waistcoat. 'After all, she did send rather a splendid wreath, didn't she?'

The little group fell silent as they remembered the lavish cross of red roses and while lilies that had brilliantly dwarfed all other tributes at the chilly graveside.

. . . Man born of a woman has but a short time to live . . .

'Of course,' began Mary, 'with Anne in Australia and you, Alex, away for so long, Liz and I felt we were always trotting off to the Grange. Dad could be very demanding. There was always something he wanted taken in, or forms he needed help filling out. He worried a lot, especially after the heart attack. Weren't we, Liz? Always off to the Grange?'

The looked-for support didn't come. Liz shook a rattle at the baby and blew into his face.

'Yes, he'd phone up, full of complaints and one of us would have to drop everything and go.' Mary sailed on, undeterred. 'And whenever we went, we couldn't get away. We'd have to listen to the same old stories about Mum over and over. There's no rest for the wicked, isn't that what they say? And the amount we must have spent in petrol these past couple of years, chasing off to see him every five minutes! Still, we mustn't begrudge it now, must we? What you might call going the extra mile?' Raising her eyebrows theatrically, she extinguished her cigarette butt with some savagery in the cut-glass ashtray on the coffee table.

'I really appreciate all you did for Dad in the last few years, both you and Lizzie.'

Alex tried to inject some warmth into her words but failed. We look like a nest of black crows, she was thinking. Her head was full of other voices and she found it hard to concentrate.

'Yes, well, we know you haven't been without your own problems,' said Adrian, shooting a warning glance at his wife.

'Metro going OK?' he queried.

'It's fine,' Alex assured him. 'Just what I had in mind. It was really good of you to arrange all that, Adrian.'

'No bother. Happy to oblige. Quite a decent service this morning, don't you think?' His question was directed at Alex, but she could only stare back at him stupidly, unable to form an answer.

. . . Like a flower he blossoms and then withers; like a shadow he flees and never stays . . .

Terry gave a gruff snorting laugh. 'Well, at least it was short! And the vicar did well – you could almost believe he'd met the old bugger!'

Mary sniffed, fingering the pearls at her neck with blood-red nails. 'Terry, really!'

'It's no use you looking at me like that. You didn't have to live with him the few years before he was put in the Grange. Lizzie and I could tell you a story or two, couldn't we?'

It was his turn to look expectantly at Lizzie, but she buried her face in the baby now gurgling on her lap.

Adrian cleared his throat. 'He had a tough life, you know. National Service as a youngster and all that. Not the opportunities then that people have today. No skills to speak of. And then being left with four girls to raise. He was old before his time. We mustn't think too harshly of him.' The young accountant pronounced his views with the authority of an elder statesman.

. . . In the midst of life we are in death: to whom can we turn

for help, but to you, Lord, who are justly angered by our sins? . . .

'Do you think the girls should be out in the garden?' ventured Lizzie. 'It's so cold and I think it's starting to rain again. I've poured orange squash for them in the kitchen.'

'Let me call them in,' suggested Alex, relieved at an opportunity to escape.

The long garden was a maze of overgrown blackberry bushes strangling nameless scrawny shrubs. At the bottom Alex could see splashes of colour in the tall grass near a couple of overturned rabbit hutches and piles of empty flowerpots.

Mary's three daughters, in ski jackets, corduroy trousers and wellingtons, were deep in some make-believe country. Their voices floated dreamily through the still November mist.

'You said I could be the mummy! I was the shop lady last time.' That was Tracey.

'OK, grumble-guts. But don't forget. If you're the mummy you have to do it properly and tell the daddy when to get out of bed to go to the office and ask him for the money to go to Sainsbury's.' Shelley was dictating terms.

'And it's my turn to make the casserole. It's chicken with Oxo cubes. And cabbage from the 'lotment.'

Little Kylie was collecting armfuls of muddy sticks and fallen leaves to fill the flowerpot kitchenware. The youngest always did the donkey work.

Alex recognized with regret her own affinity with Shelley's dominance.

'But why do you always have to be the teacher? I can read now and do sums,' Mary used to whine, often enough.

'You know why,' Alex would snap back. 'I can do magic.

That's why. Tell Annie and Lizzie to bring those boxes to make the school.'

'I can do magic.'

A few sleight-of-hand devices maintained her early hold over her sisters, then later there was the easy superiority of the grammar-school place. They marvelled at her tricks with coins and rings and coloured cotton squares. The skills practised in the den in the bottom of the garden stood her in good stead as she slipped the chocolate, the marshmallows, the lipsticks, into her pocket, up her sleeve, between the textbooks in her school bag.

'Shelley, it's time to come in.'

'Do we have to?' the child replied, her lower lip pouting. 'It's more fun out here.'

But she skipped off up the path, followed by Tracey.

Kylie slipped her hand into Alex's and looked up at her, frowning.

'Aunty Alex?'

'Yes, what is it?'

'Mummy said she don't know if Grandad went up to heaven. She said he didn't keep none of the rules. About being good and that. But he did give me a 50p lots of times, didn't he? And last Christmas he gave me a Sindy doll, didn't he? And what's going to happen to all Grandad's bottles with halfpennies in because Mummy said there's not going to be any halfpennies anymore, it said on the news, and no halfpenny chews. And Mummy said you prob'ly had to be ever so, ever so good, to go to heaven. Did Uncle Peter go to heaven? Daddy said Uncle Peter must've been a bad driver but that's not the same as being a bad man, is it, Aunty Alex?'

Alex took a deep breath and crouched down till she was on a level with the troubled blue eyes.

'Kylie, it's not doing lots of good things that gets us a place in heaven, you know.'

'Isn't it?'

'Not really. The important thing is getting to know the only good person there is, Jesus. And when we love him and want to follow him, of course we want to do good things to be like him because he's sort of our best friend. But heaven . . . well, heaven comes as a sort of wonderful free gift when we believe in Jesus and decide he's going to be our best friend.'

Alex studied the little face. The Travers eyes, but Adrian's thin pale blond hair, square face and dimpled chin. She was glad the child looked like her father. Like some police Identikit, she'd often pieced together different combinations of her own features with Peter's, wondering what the genetic gamble would produce if they had a child. And generally she would opt in her daydreams for a result that largely favoured Peter, conjuring a little boy with a wide slow smiling mouth and straight blond hair that flopped wayward over grey-green eyes. But that was one magic trick that hadn't worked. No comparison, really, with what they had been offered.

Inside, over fruitcake and cups of tea, there was some bickering about family photograph albums, and then an old dressing-table. The discussions were apparently friendly, but there was an undercurrent of greed that appalled Alex. There was also the insinuation that Alex had lost any claim to Dad's pathetic bits and pieces by leaving the country and not being on hand when needed. Terry looked aggressive, and Mary used the phrase 'Charity begins at home' more than once without explaining quite what she meant. But everyone recognized it as a complaint against Alex's absence.

'Naturally, you'll keep most of Dad's things, Liz,' said Mary, magnanimously. 'After all, this is your home. That would be fair and proper. I was just wondering about the old clock in the hall. It was Aunty Betty's, wasn't it? Adrian's got a colleague at the office who knows about these things. We wouldn't mind spending a bit on having it done up, you know, get it going, just as a keepsake. It would look rather nice on our landing, we thought.'

Lizzie smiled, rocking absent-mindedly as she offered a bottle to the baby. 'Of course, please take it. What about you, Alex, would you . . .?'

Alex shook her head. Mary smiled and lit another cigarette.

. . . earth to earth, ashes to ashes, dust to dust . . .

Mentally Alex was lingering at the graveside, watching the rivulets of rain run over the spade slices of yellow clay, and the mud splashes splatter on the vicar's hemline. The small, pathetic family of black crows huddled under umbrellas. What holds us together? Alex had wondered then. Sharing a womb that later rejected us? And yet somehow it's a hold that's unbreakable. We're bone of her bone, flesh of her flesh, fruit of his semen. Multiplying cells grown from their acts of love or lust, however unthinking. Though our destinies are all so different, the blood-line chains us together.

In the graveside tableau, Mary blew her nose into a lace handkerchief and leaned on Adrian's arm. Adrian stood solid and unperturbable, his face a mask. Terry was openly bored. A few yards away, on the path, a row of ghostly faces belonging to young Lizzie and the children pressed against the car window. Alex wondered if Sister Hendry might have been there, but obviously duty did not go that far. It was not a very fond farewell.

None of the family had attended either the cremation or the thanksgiving service for Peter earlier that year in Hong Kong. She hadn't wanted them there, so it had been a relief to accept that the cost of the flight alone would be enough to provide them an escape.

Richard had helped her put together the order of service. Though still dreaming through the days, she was sufficiently aware to insist it was to be a simple but sincere celebration of life rather than a commemoration of death. The church was packed with friends and colleagues. Project teams from all over Asia sent representatives; those that couldn't, sent messages to be read. Kind messages with no need to search for inane generalities. There was music. Yes, there were tears, but there was also a kind of bedrock of confidence that almost warmed Alex's frigid heart. It certainly comforted her in retrospect even though her appreciation at the time was limited.

. . . in sure and certain hope of the resurrection to eternal life . . .

Of course, it was the hope that made the difference. Though torn from her, savagely, by some circumstances cruelly incomprehensible, there was the hope that amounted by faith to an unshakeable conviction. Peter was not annihilated but transported to some indescribably better place.

Alex recalled that strange sensation of confusion during the thanksgiving service when for a split second she thought she was at a wedding and waiting for the question to be asked about any man knowing any just impediment. Was someone going to ask the question about impediments to Peter being released to death, to heaven, to eternity? But her permission was not sought, so there was no opportunity to speak out and withhold it.

How thankful she was for the hope of reunion!

And how many times had she longed to artificially contrive that reunion? She would admit it to no other, but to God confessed it and felt no shame in it, secure in some instinct that in his eyes this disgrace was less dreadful than others made it out to be. God understood her longing to hasten the day, whereas others might shudder and be shocked at the suggestion. She knew that a walk by the Avon would be accompanied today with perhaps more courage than in past days, so she avoided it studiously. Would they blame her mother for that? Should she? Was there some inherited weakness? Whatever, such temptation regularly presented itself, in varying guises, but particularly in the form of easy, innocuous-looking white pills. So pleasant, it would be, to sleep so deep and dreamless and wake so eagerly.

Yes, there was the ever-present hope of reunion. It was something to hold on to. Sometimes, it was everything.

My ingratitude is so immense, please forgive me, Father, Jehovah Shammah, the Lord who is there.

She needed to keep a realistic hold on Peter in her mind and heart, see him as he was. Not make him into some plaster saint. What was the worst she could summon up to convict her husband? Let her not forget the blemishes. She searched her memories. Careless. He lost things – anything from reports left in airport lounges and buttons off shirts to umbrellas on taxi seats and library books forgotten in hotel rooms. Bad timekeeper. He was often late for meetings and it was only due to her nagging he hadn't missed several planes. Forgetful. He rarely remembered her birthday without a prompt.

Staring out of the window at Stonebridge Road, Alex dredged up the little niggling faults. She dare not list his qualities today or she would be overwhelmed. She knew with sudden conviction that even in the black tunnelled grief of early widowhood she had so much more than these strangers to whom she was indeed tied by blood. Buried deep down by pain, but not lost, were rivers of joy and peace waiting to rise on the spring tide. Today she couldn't even envy them their children. She would not exchange an absent Peter for others whom she saw – alive but unfaithful, alive but unloving, alive but all those other things that Peter had not been.

And, knowing all that, she asked herself, wasn't it time to put off the self-absorption that walled her in along with only nightmares for company?

TWELVE

Up here the wind was king. It raced exulting over the flat hilltop and swooped over the edge, roaring unchecked down through the Vale of the White Horse.

Alex struck the white chalk with the toe of her boot. Legend had it that if you stood in the eye of the mystical white horse and wished . . .

But that was just as effective as biting into a mince pie.

She lifted her eyes to the enormity of the panorama. Fat grey clouds were being buffeted through the skies. One or two circling rooks. And as far as she could see in all directions stretched blankets of ploughed fields hemmed with the grey lines of dry-stone walls. A few scattered copses. And the postcard villages hibernating, dreaming through the first day of December, the ribbon roads empty. No sound but the moan of the wind.

Apparent peace. She supposed that a chance walker might look at her and decide she, too, was at peace. But how deeply did that peace hold true? Not many miles away, perhaps in the midst of similarly tranquil country scenery, two striking miners had been charged last night with the murder of a taxi-driver killed when a breeze-block had been thrown through his windscreen from a bridge. Alex felt a chill pass through her as she listened to radio reports of violence on the picket lines. And she recognized a bitterness not far removed just under the surface of her own skin.

As it happened, the ancient fort site was deserted today. No serious ramblers with dogs racing in circles. No families with kites on strings. Just a few sheep, their wool greasy and tattered, crudely raddled, chewing philosophically around four or five small square plots roped off for a student dig.

The cold was defeating her. Alex returned to the Metro, and poured tea from her flask. She reached into her pocket and pulled out the envelope. She unfolded the drawing and studied it again. Energetic scribbles, mostly in red crayon, some stick-like limbs in pencil. 'Me and red shoes' read the ungainly caption underneath.

Then Alex read, for the ninth or tenth time, the note from Sister Bridget. It was unsatisfactorily brief. And cautious. Since Alex had asked, Siu Ling was in reasonably good health. She'd had a cold, but was over it. The last routine hearing tests were more optimistic. True, she had been rather moody and difficult in recent months, reminiscent of her arrival at Joyful Haven. Uncooperative with the speech therapist. Probably just a phase, Sister Bridget concluded, with uncharacteristic vagueness. They all felt she needed more social interaction and had been successful in getting an English-medium reception class at a local school to give her a place three mornings a week from the New Year, on an experimental basis at first.

Like most strong, direct characters, Sister Bridget was transparent. Alex suspected that her old friend was tempering what she said in some way. Did that mean that she felt that giving her information about Siu Ling was not wise? Or did it mean that the child was in fact unhappy, or worse, but that she didn't want Alex to feel responsible in any way?

Strangely, it was a guilt Alex had never shouldered. For perhaps the first time, she contemplated the possibility that the accident and her abrupt disappearance from Joyful Haven might have had repercussions on Siu Ling. She'd always believed that the stoical little creature, who'd never showed any signs of missing her when she was away, had a supreme acceptance of the way things were day to day that precluded many normal emotions. Had she been wrong about that? She conjured up an image of the little girl's moon-shaped face, placid and a little wistful, the dark eyes staring into middle distance.

Alex noticed with surprise that the light was failing, and drove back to the village, parking outside the minimart to buy milk and bread. As she was about to get back into the car to drive off, she saw Mandy coming out of the Post Office and knew she ought to wait.

'Hi! What have you done with the kids this afternoon?'

'My Mum's here from Gloucester for a few days.'

'That's nice.'

'She goes back on the coach tomorrow morning.'

Mandy looked lost, biting her lower lip. Alex searched desperately for words to continue the conversation.

'Look, about the other day, the babysitting, I'm really sorry I . . .'

'Oh, that's nothing. Forget it. Really, that's fine.'

Alex forced a smile.

'Babysitting's not my thing. I'm not really that good with children.'

'I expect you're really glad you haven't got any. In the circumstances.'

Mandy's words knocked the breath out of her. She swallowed hard.

'I mean, because of losing your husband,' faltered Mandy, searching Alex's eyes. 'You know, being stuck on your own, with a few kids, that would be hard. Wouldn't it?'

'I expect so,' answered Alex, faintly.

'God, I've really put my foot in it now, haven't I? Saying that? I'm really sorry.' Mandy was in a panic, the words a torrent. 'It's just . . . it's just . . . that was exactly what was on my mind, coming out of the Post Office, thinking about things, the way they are right now, and even wishing I didn't have the kids, wishing I was far away, or someone else.'

Suddenly, horrifyingly, she burst into tears, clutching blindly for Alex's hand.

Quickly Alex reached up and stroked the fluffy ginger curls.

'What's wrong, Mandy? What's happened? Come on. Get in the car. Come home with me for a cup of tea. Will your Mum be OK with the children for a little while longer?' She spoke instinctively.

Mandy nodded, wiping her face with the back of her hand. Alex unlocked the car and Mandy slipped into the passenger seat, her head slumped forward.

Alex wished the cottage was more welcoming. She put the lights on, pulled the curtains across and rushed up the stairs to turn up the central heating before putting the kettle on to make tea.

'Let me take your coat. The radiators will start warming up any minute. Sorry, I don't have any biscuits.'

'It's Shaun. He's got himself into trouble, and I don't think I can cope with it any more.' Mandy wasted no words on preamble. She perched on the edge of the sofa, twisting a tissue in her fingers.

'He's been taking money from the garage. Not small amounts. Fifty pounds here, a hundred there. His Dad's never been very bright at the book-keeping side of the business and thought at first he'd made some mistakes himself adding things up. Then he thought it was Lucy, the young girl on the counter there, so he started watching her, staying behind to spy on her cashing up at the end of the day and so on. And then last week . . .'

Her voice trailed off as fresh tears came.

'Go on,' said Alex gently, squeezing her arm.

'If he knew I was here, telling someone . . .'

'I won't repeat a word to anyone, you know that.'

Mandy took a deep breath.

'Well, it's worse. It's a lot worse than just a bit of pilfering. Last week his Dad actually caught him out. Shaun was getting a customer to write a cheque out to him personally, not the business, and Shaun . . . well, he broke down then and there. He's always been that close to his Dad, more so than his Mum really, especially since he left school and went into the business. He told his Dad everything, and then his Dad came round straight away to tell me. Shaun couldn't face me on his own. The reason he'd been taking the money was to pay off these gambling debts he's run up.'

'Gambling!' Alex blurted out the exclamation and then tried to disguise her shock.

Mandy shrugged.

'Yeah, well, even before we were married I knew Shaun had a weakness for betting on the horses. Of course, then it didn't matter that much, a few pounds a week when we were both working was OK. But after I fell pregnant with Stephen, which was pretty soon after we got married, and I had to give up my job at the building society, I told him then and there he'd have to give it up. Well, you have to make sacrifices when you have children, don't you?'

Alex nodded, dumbly.

'He did for a while. Give it up, I mean. Apart from if there was some special race on, like the Derby. Then, just over two years ago, when I was expecting Darren it would have been, some mates called at the flat for him one day and said they were part of his syndicate, and come to collect their winnings. Seems he'd organized some local syndicate, based on half a dozen garages in the villages round here.'

'And that was the first you knew of it?'

'Yeah. He refused to give it up. According to him he was never going to get rich working for his Dad, the business was never going to be any bigger in a village this size and this . . . this sideline, he called it, was going to bring in some big money sooner or later that would really set us up. We'd be able to put a deposit on our own hone, he said. And then he'd give up the syndicate, but not before.'

'I guess things haven't worked out like that,' prompted Alex, gently.

'No,' Mandy sighed. 'Seems he didn't place some of the bets one week, and used the money himself to bet on another horse he'd had a tip-off was a dead cert. Well, you can guess what happened. His horse fell at the first fence, and two of his mates had picked the winner. Since then he's been struggling to put things straight, borrowing from the till at the garage, always thinking the next win will be the big one that will mean he can pay everyone off. But he's been getting into a deeper and deeper mess.

'It all explains why money's tighter than ever and we've had some really terrible rows these past few months. Like when I told him last week I needed some money to get Darren some new shoes. He just hit the roof. I've never seen him so mad. I was scared he was going to hit me, or the kids.'

'But he didn't, did he?'

'No. Not yet.' She pulled another tissue from her pocket and dabbed at her eyes.

'But I just don't know him any more. He's not the man I married. I tell you, Alex, I keep thinking I can't go on like this much longer. I've begged him to change. Today, in the Post Office, I saw this headline. You know, the story in the newspaper abut that woman in the TV quiz show who's walked out on her husband and four kids? And I was thinking . . . I was thinking, "Good luck to her." I was thinking, I should do the same. This gambling, it's like some sort of disease that can't be cured and I don't want to live with it for the rest of my life. I could do the same as she did. Just pack a bag and walk out. Go. Start a new life. I had a word with Sally, the manageress at the building society. Phoned her yesterday. She'll give me a good reference. I was there over five years. They've got branches all over the place. Maybe . . .'

'But what about Stephen and Darren?'

Mandy was suddenly hostile.

'Well, that's the tough bit. Don't think it's not tearing me apart to think about leaving them. But I wouldn't be able to do anything if I had them with me, would I? Darren's too little for playgroup even. Perhaps Shaun's Mum could have them for a while. Or maybe they could live with my Mum in Gloucester for a bit. I could get a job, get back on my feet. Mum's ever so good with them. Later . . .'

'But, Mandy, it's not the same for kids to be brought . . .'

'It's no fun for them now, Alex, not living with us fighting and quarrelling all the time!' Mandy interrupted, roused to anger.

'And sooner or later Shaun's going to do one of them some harm when that bad temper gets the better of him. What kind of life do the kids have now? What kind of future?'

She sank her face on to her hands.

A sudden thought struck Alex.

'But Mandy, what about the new baby? Didn't you tell me you were pregnant?'

Looking up, Mandy flushed scarlet.

'Oh God, did I tell you about that?' she stammered.

'Yes, that day we met in the minimart. Remember?'

'Look, don't tell anyone about that, Alex. Promise? If Mum finds out, she'll kill me. The thing is, that's where I went the other night, the night I wanted you to babysit. I went to the evening surgery to see that new woman doctor, Dr Taylor. 'Course, I was really excited when I knew I was pregnant again. But when I started thinking about it . . . this is the worst time to be thinking of having another baby. I explained it all to Dr Taylor, that it was really a mistake. She's written me a letter of referral, to the clinic in Oxford, you know . . .'

Her voice had diminished to a whisper.

'Oh, Mandy! Does Shaun . . . does he want that, too?'

'Not at first. He was dead against it. But when I told him it might be all over between us anyway, he said he didn't care, it was up to me.' Mandy's lips trembled and she lowered her head.

Alex's mind was racing. She felt she had no answers but

154

that there ought to be some. There ought to be something that could be said, something that could be done, to avert the break-up of this family.

She began hesitantly.

'Mandy, I just don't know what to say. Not yet. But there is some way out of this. There must be. We just have to find the way out. I need a bit of time to think about it.'

Mandy lifted her head and shook her curls, looking bewildered, exhausted.

'I shouldn't have bothered you with all this. I hardly know you.' Her voice was flat and dull now. 'You must have enough problems of your own.'

'No. You should have bothered me. Friends need to bother each other all the time with their problems, share them, help each other work out some answers. I'm really glad you've talked to me about it.' She almost choked on her own words, knowing how far she was from taking her own advice. The thing was, she realized she did believe in what she was saying.

The two sat silent, reflective for a few seconds.

'Here, your tea's getting cold. Drink up and I'll run you home. But I want you to promise me you won't do anything rash. Your kids need you. And so does your husband. Would you let me come and see you tomorrow afternoon when I've had a chance to think about things?'

'I can't see it'll do any good,' said Mandy, getting to her feet.

'Well, we'll see about that. You live round the corner from the Swan, don't you? Can I come to see you around three?'

'It's flat 17B. Make it nearer four, then I'll be back from collecting Stephen from playgroup.'

155

'Four it is. And, Mandy, will you promise? You know, to still be there?'

'Promise.'

Life was full of echoes, thought Alex, later. If only I hadn't stopped at the minimart on the way back from the White Horse Hill, if I hadn't paused when I'd seen Mandy . . .

Now, suddenly, she was committed in a situation in which she felt desperately out of her depth. There was a theory, wasn't there, that history was like a coiled spring, with all the events happening here and now, all at once. She felt her own place in history was so fragile she kept slipping off her place on the coil, bumping into parallel roads and losing her way. Or was it that the earthquake of Peter's death had ripped up the road and sent it sprawling like a concertina into other roads already travelled or yet to come?

Mandy needed more than sticking-plaster remedies. And Alex knew if she was to be any help to the young mother she must sort out some of the jumble of her own emotions first.

She'd been amazed at her reaction of distaste to the story of Shaun's involvement in gambling, and hoped it hadn't been too evident in her face. May God forgive her for the anger and disgust against a young man she'd hardly met that had welled up from somewhere deep inside, so bitter to the taste it was frightening. She must have walked that road on the coil of history before.

She struggled in her memories, looking for the links, and eventually found one. The picture became clearer. Two raised voices. His was strident, defensive, out of control, running on and on as he stood in the doorway, his donkey jacket hanging open over the stained blue overalls. Hers was appealing, hesitant, stumbling, but less out of control, steeled with a determination born of desperation. Leaning on the old stove for support, she waved at him the pile of yellow tickets she'd found behind the bedroom clock, contemptuously reading out the ridiculous names of the greyhounds, naming his folly. She challenged, talked of the simple needs of her four little girls, more daring than she'd ever been even though there were tears glittering in her eyes. He slammed the back door, strode into the kitchen, pushed her aside and flung himself down at the kitchen table. His voice rose through denial to excuse, then lowered to conciliation and hollow promises.

Peering through the banisters, shivering and hungry, little Alex fed on every word, storing some away against future understanding.

Until now she'd forgotten the humiliation of seeming to count for less than a dog to her father. He was a victim, too, of course. Slave to a passion that dominated him for years and kept the family on the breadline. And she'd forgotten the fleeting bravery of her mother, a wounded bear defending her cubs against the wolf she took to her bed. Alex suddenly felt a surge of warmth for Lizzie Travers. Almost love.

There was another horror she needed to name in Mandy's story. That was closer to home. She didn't need to search far for it. It was the searing anger she felt towards a young woman who could even consider arresting the miracle of multiplying cells going on within her own body. It was an irony she'd met before, of course, and thrown at God repeatedly. What kind of justice was it that someone like Mandy was blessed with an easy, unthinking fertility? While others . . .?

That night, the loneliness was intense. Not just the

absence of a lover's caress, but the hunger for a mother's goodnight kiss, a father's nod of approval, a child's outreaching arms. Alex drew the sleeping-bag tightly round her and accused herself of drowning in sentiment and self-pity, but was not convinced or comforted.

THIRTEEN

Swan Court was a low red-brick block, unadorned and unappealing. The cut-and-thrust lines of the mid 1970s looked stark and shabby after a decade of use and abuse. The building crouched behind the Swan public house on the edge of the village, seemingly embarrassed at its own incongruity.

Alex arrived breathless at the door of flat 17B, having decided at the last moment to walk rather than drive. Ten past four. She rang the bell.

'Oh, here you are! I wondered . . . well, I was thinking you might have changed your mind about coming.' Mandy motioned her to come in.

'No. Sorry I'm a bit late.'

In the living-room four-year-old Stephen was sitting at the table behind a plate of fish fingers and chips. He paused briefly, his fork in mid-air, to eye Alex with some suspicion, but soon continued eating.

'He's always starving when he gets in from playgroup,' explained Mandy, apologetically.

Alex took in the cramped room at a glance. Under the window, Darren was sitting in a cot, surrounded by toys. He was stabbing his fingers at a musical box which was tinkling the approximate notes of 'Row, row, row the boat'.

More toys littered the rug in front of the gas fire on the wall. A large copper-coloured fire-guard was hung with washing. There was a low three-piece suite in dark green PVC, a TV and a pile of magazines on a long teak coffee table, a Formica-topped table and four chairs.

Mandy appeared with two mugs.

'Go ahead, sit down. Is coffee all right? I'm out of teabags. I meant to call in at the mimimart on the way back this afternoon but I completely forgot.'

She balanced the mugs next to the sugar bowl on the pile of magazines. She looked calmer than yesterday, but pale and apprehensive.

'You must think I'm a real idiot, breaking down on you yesterday. I'm not sure what came over me,' she began, stirring her coffee.

'Well, it's understandable. You've got a lot on your mind right now.'

'Stephen, love, have you finished? Get the flannel from the kitchen and wipe your hands. And then you can play with the Lego in the bedroom.'

Stephen slid off his chair and stared at Alex.

'Don't want to, Mummy. Want to watch TV.'

'Later. First I want you to see if you can finish that aeroplane we started together.'

'OK. Wheeeeee!' Stephen stuck his arms out and flew his body out of the room and along the hall.

Mandy sighed. 'He's a good kid really. Loves playgroup.'

Alex sensed that Mandy was letting her off the hook. It would be all right to say nothing about yesterday's

160

revelations, to sweep them under the carpet, to talk about the children, the weather, anything. And she was tempted.

'How did you meet Shaun?' asked Alex abruptly.

There was no answer. Mandy stared frowning into her mug, clasping it with both hands.

'Mandy?'

'Yes,' she replied at last. 'Sorry. For a moment I was miles away. It was about six years ago. At Silver Blades, the ice-rink in Bristol. Shaun had come with a group from the church youth club. He didn't go to the youth club usually, but his Dad used to let the club have the use of the minibus he kept at the garage, for their outings. He didn't charge them anything, except petrol. And the vicar, not the one we've got now, the one before, he kept on inviting Shaun to go along. Eventually, one night he did! And that was one of the nights I was there. I used to take the coach to Bristol some Friday nights after school to spend the weekend at my Aunty Margaret's and go skating with my cousins, especially if Mum was working late shifts at the weekend.'

'So you bumped into each other on the ice?'

'Nothing as romantic! No. There were these lockers along one side of the rink where you could leave your shoes while you put the hire skates on. I put 10p in mine and it got jammed. I was thumping it, and Shaun came up and offered to help.'

'To rescue a damsel in distress!'

'Well, to save a damsel wasting 10p, anyway!' Mandy laughed.

'What did you like about him, when you first met him?'

'Hard to say. It wasn't good looks or a big bank balance! He was shy. Thoughtful. Not cocky, like lots of the other

161

boys around. Clever with his hands. Sort of natural, too. He didn't try to impress anyone. I liked the way he was fond of his parents.'

'I guess that, underneath it all, Shaun is still all those things? Still all those things that made him the person you first loved?' suggested Alex.

Mandy looked at her, quizzical, her lips tightening into a hard line.

'Alex, you don't know what he's been like these past few months! Bad-tempered, shouting at me and the kids at the slightest thing. Touchy isn't the word for it! He's stormed out of the house once or twice when I've tried to talk to him about the gambling.'

Alex took a deep breath.

'I don't know Shaun, so you would be the best judge of what's going on in his life. But I do know a bit about gambling and the stresses it puts on a person, the way it can change someone, alter a personality.'

Mandy stared. Her eyes were troubled. Deep down, she wants to believe again in her husband, thought Alex. And that understanding gave her the courage to go on.

'Take my Dad. He used to gamble when we were little. Greyhounds were his weakness. I can remember some tremendous shouting matches. Fights. Sometimes Mum would walk out. We were always hard up and mostly because of the betting. There were other things, of course, like Dad never being able to keep any kind of job for more than a year or so before having a row with the foreman or something like that.

'I never really thought about *why* he was gambling. Just saw it as part of the bad side of his character. Since the funeral I've been wondering more. In a way you never really know your own parents, do you? All you really know

162

is the little lopsided role they play in your life, and you don't always understand that.

'I've been trying to picture Dad as a young man with no job security, no skills, not much experience except a couple of years of Army life. From the bits I remember Mum telling me, he was a bit of a clown when she first met him. Always good for a laugh. Then, things changed. Life got serious. What was it like for him, getting a young woman pregnant and suddenly being tied down, trying to support a wife and then a baby, and pretty soon another on the way? Must have been a bit of a shock for him, a struggle. I don't know. I can only guess at the kind of stresses going on inside. Perhaps he began to feel resentful about what he'd given up, even though he loved his wife and kids in his own way, perhaps feeling claustrophobic now and again, wanting to escape but not being able to. Swallowing the lie that says a bit of money brings you instant freedom. That's where the greyhounds came in. The race track was somewhere to go on a Saturday night, where he had his own circle of friends, could have a few beers and forget the rest of the week. And where he could forget he had a wife at home desperately trying to make ends meet, to feed and clothe the children.'

'Are you saying that me and the kids are doing that to Shaun? Tying him down and that? But it's not like that.' Mandy's voice was strained.

'I'm just trying to tell you the kind of pressures that gambling put our family under.'

The toddler stood up, rattling the cot bars and whimpering.

'I need to get Darren a drink.'

Alex followed Mandy into the kitchen.

'Mandy, look, what I'm trying to say is, that the stresses come, and it's no crime that we don't always cope as well as we should. Sometimes we all feel the weight of our responsibilities, making us feel that we've lost our freedom. That could be what's happening to Shaun. It happens to us all at times. What about you? Don't you feel a bit imprisoned sometimes? Trapped?' Alex made an effort to keep her voice low and even.

Mandy shook her head impatiently, leaning over the sink, filling a plastic cup with blackcurrant juice.

She turned on Alex, her voice suddenly strident.

'OK. Maybe. Maybe I feel like I'm in a prison in this damn flat, stuck in a dead village in the back of beyond. But I don't go mad or daft, do I? I don't go out and spend the housekeeping at the races. I don't run up debts. Do I? I don't help myself to money from the till. Do I?'

And now Alex couldn't resist the challenge thrown down. She rushed in, her sudden fluency like a knife.

'No. Under pressure you do different things. You think about leaving home and getting a job like you used to before you were married. You think about leaving your husband and taking your kids to live with your Mum. You even . . . you think about ending a defenceless life!'

Mandy let the cup drop, clutching with both hands on the edge of the sink and leaning forward. The blackcurrant ran in rivers down the stainless-steel draining-board. A sob broke from her throat.

'I think you'd better go,' she gasped. 'Please. Go now!'

Without a word, Alex let herself out of the flat. The street lamps filtered cheerlessly through the early evening gloom as she trudged back to the cottage, slow and burdened.

Well, she'd made a real mess of that! What right had she to play amateur psychologist, anyway? If anyone needed analysing it was her, Alex, not Mandy.

Feeling that the makeshift bridge between her and

Mandy had been washed away on a high tide of crude good intentions, she tried to dismiss the conversation from her mind. But little scattered phrases were indelible and re-ran with all the accompanying Technicolor emotions of resentment, distress, anger.

Early the next morning, she was listlessly thumbing through the local paper at the kitchen table when the phone rang.

'Alex? It's me. Mandy.'

'Oh, hi!' Alex tried to focus her mind, and feigned casual cheerfulness as a first defence.

'I need to apologize. I feel really bad about telling you to leave yesterday.'

'No, please. It wasn't your fault. I was being a bit . . . well, a bit blunt. Too hard on you. I should be the one to apologize. I'm sorry.'

'Yes, well, you were a bit blunt. But perhaps it was for the best. The thing is, I've been thinking over what you said. Been awake most of the night, actually. You've got a point, about gambling. I've never really stopped to think about *why* Shaun's been doing it. You could be right about him feeling under pressure, a bit cramped. Life's a bit of a treadmill at the moment, if you want the truth. You know, money short, him working long hours and me stuck at home with the kids. When he gets home, I'm tired, fed up . . . All sorts of dreams we had when we were first married . . .' Her voice wavered.

'Dreams are important, but . . .'

'Yeah, well, the dreams just haven't come true and somehow we've stopped believing they'll ever happen, so there's nothing to look forward to. Nothing.'

'I've just had an idea.' Alex broke the short awkward silence. 'I've just been looking through the *Star*. How would you like to go into Swindon this afternoon? There's some grand arrival of Father Christmas and his elves or some such nonsense, switching on the Christmas lights and then a parade past the shops into the grotto in Debenhams. I was thinking Stephen would enjoy it. What do you think?' She held her breath.

'He'd love it! That would be really great.'

Alex released the breath slowly. Thank you, Father, for being the God of second chances.

The shopping precinct was seasonably colourful and the crowds possessed of an unusual *bonhomie*.

'Here, come on, squeeze though this gap with the kids.' An enormous barrel of a woman in a fluorescent plaid scarf made way for Alex carrying Darren, Mandy with Stephen in tow. They edged through in front of her. A crackling PA system was churning out 'Rudolf the Rednosed Reindeer' and Santa himself was swaying to the beat, tapping his black wellingtons on a makeshift dais. Behind him a sleigh was liberally decorated with wedges of cotton wool and white polystyrene chips.

'Mummy, has Santa got my letter already? Does he know what I want?'

'Oh, he's sure to have got it by now. Don't you think so, Alex?' smiled Mandy.

Alex nodded and returned the smile, shifting Darren on to her other arm. He was heavy, bundled in padded anorak, fur-trimmed hood and mitts. His head rolled against her shoulder and his eyelids fluttered sleepily.

'Mummy, mummy, look! Are they angels?' shouted Stephen, hopping up and down.

'Hard to say. But they could be,' Mandy assured him.

The stage area was besieged by an army of children dressed unpractically in flowing lengths of white nylon net, pink tights, ballet shoes and tinselled headdresses. They were carrying miniature red felt sacks full of boiled sweets and lollipops which they began distributing freely to the children in the waiting crowd. Stephen soon had both pockets and both hands full. Santa took the microphone and began extolling the virtues of certain shops in the precinct, reading out the extravaganza of special offers from a curled scroll. After that, a troupe of handbell ringers took to the stage for a performance of 'O Little Town of Bethlehem' that made up in enthusiasm for what it lacked in musicality.

'Shall I take Darren now? He must be making your arms ache. I knew we should have brought the buggy,' said Mandy.

'No, leave him for a while, I think he's dropping off to sleep. And I don't think we could have managed the buggy, not in these crowds.'

'Let's go for a cup of tea, shall we?' suggested Mandy, a few minutes later. 'I think Stephen's seen enough of Santa for the moment. If we take a break now, by the time we get to the grotto maybe the crowds will have thinned a bit.'

At a corner table in the Swiss Chalet, Stephen solemnly admired his gingerbread man with Smartie buttons while sucking orange juice up a straw. Darren sprawled rosy-cheeked and insensible on Mandy's lap.

'I'm going to talk to him about it tonight. Have it out with him,' announced Mandy without warning.

'What?'

'Shaun. I've decided I'm going to talk to him about the money. And, well, other things. We've not been talking things over properly for a long time. Shouting, yes. But talking, no. That's part of the problem.' She gave a wry smile and shook her head, the amber curls trembling.

'That sounds a good idea. If you think you're ready for it. Take it carefully.' Alex spoke hesitantly.

'I realized, last night after you'd gone, I've not been looking at things, you know, deep enough. I've been looking at the things that show, not the things, the reasons behind them. And that's been making me see Shaun as some kind of enemy against me and the kids. Do you know what I mean?'

She sighed in frustration. 'I can't really explain. I'm not good with words, like you are. We need to make some plans, about sorting out the debt. And you're right about the real Shaun not being bad-tempered. It must be the debt and everything making him behave like this, out of character.'

'Tackling the problem together could make all the difference. If Shaun knows you're on his side, well, that could really help. What does Shaun's Dad say about what he owes the garage?' asked Alex.

'He'd write it off if he could. But I think we need to pay it all back. It's the principle of the thing, isn't it? And pay off the debts Shaun owes the others in the syndicate. It's not going to be easy. Perhaps his Dad will let us pay things off bit by bit out of his wages.'

She reddened and bit her lip before continuing slowly. 'And, Alex, I want you to know . . . I called the clinic. First thing this morning. I cancelled the appointment. I'm not sure I could really have gone through with it anyway. I couldn't have lived with myself if I had. I was trying not to think about, you know, what it really meant. You forced me to face up to it. I was awake all last night, couldn't stop thinking about the . . . our baby. I can't do it.' She shook her head.

Alex felt tears prickling her eyes.

'Oh, Mandy,' she whispered. 'I was so clumsy and hard on you. But you seem to have worked it all out in spite of me. You really have had a tough night. So, you're really prepared to give it another try?'

'I suppose so. But a lot depends on Shaun. I'm going to be straight with him. It all depends on how much effort he's prepared to put into sorting things out and making a real effort to control the gambling.'

'I'm so glad! I'm sure you won't regret trying to put things back together again.' Alex reached over the table and squeezed Mandy's hand. The God of second chances was able to give others grace to give second chances.

After a visit to Santa's grotto, Stephen came away beaming and clutching a red and silver plastic sword.

'He *did* get the letter! He said so. He said he's got hundreds and millions of letters. This sword wasn't on my list, Mummy, but he said this was extra. He said if I was a good boy I'd get lots and lots of presents on Christmas Day.'

Daylight had long gone and a light drizzle just beginning when they reached the car park. Alex strapped Stephen into the front passenger seat while Mandy wrestled Darren and half a dozen plastic bags into the back seat.

'It's really good of you to let me stop off at Sainsbury's,' said Mandy. 'This lot should keep us going for a few days. It's really tough struggling to and from the minimart every day, balancing bags on the buggy. And it's been great to have a few hours break away from the flat and the village.'

'I wish I'd thought of taking you shopping before. Really, it's no bother.'

'I hope we get home before Shaun finishes work. I've just

realized I didn't leave a note of where we were going, and I'm not sure he took his keys this morning.'

'It shouldn't take us much more than twenty-five minutes, as long as the traffic's reasonable.'

But the traffic wasn't reasonable. After queuing to get out of the car park they joined a slow snake of cars shuffling up to a major roundabout. Beyond that, things didn't improve much.

'I'll try going the back way,' Alex decided, indicating left.

The town finally behind them, the pace quickened. But the rain, too, accelerated, cutting down visibility. Alex gripped the wheel tightly and leaned forward.

'What rain! Like stair-rods, my mother would say,' commented Mandy. 'Stephen, be a good boy. Sit still!'

'Swish, swoosh, swish, swoosh,' chanted Stephen, in time with the wipers. He swayed from side to side and began to slice the plastic sword through the air.

'Swish, swoosh.'

'Stephen, I said sit still! And put your toy down till we get home. Or else!'

The warning came in vain or too late. One of the swipes with the sword picked up the epaulette on Alex's raincoat and tugged. Alex felt the sudden wrenching at her shoulder at the same time as her eyes were transfixed by the flash of red. The steering-wheel wavered in her uncertain grasp and she pressed violently on the brakes. The Metro slewed to a halt, nearside wheels spinning on a muddy verge and front bumper just brushing the stiff branches of a bare hawthorn hedge. From the back seat came a piercing scream as Darren woke with a jolt. The toy sword clattered down somewhere near the gear stick.

'It's all right, Darren. Ssh. Everything's fine. Just a little bump,' soothed Mandy, automatically, her voice shocked and slow. 'Stephen, are you OK, love?'

Stephen, his eyes wide, nodded. He wrapped his arms around his chest and shrank back against the seat.

Alex began to shake.

FOURTEEN

'A perfect baby? But Alex, you know, there's really no such thing!' said Helen, sighing.

It was later that evening. Alex sat at the applewood table, a blanket around her shoulders, staring into the swirls of a wood knot.

The trembling had not gone away. She struggled to piece together the last few hours. She understood that she'd slipped off the time coil to rehearse again that most dreadful of days. The pattern of the real day had been so full of echoes that the here and now had become pale and swallowed up. Chinese New Year had burst out to trample on Christmas. How long she sat in the car staring out at the hawthorn bush which had regularly and persistently metamorphosed into an impenetrable grey wall, she wasn't sure. Dimly she was aware of Mandy shaking her by the shoulder, calling her name along a tunnel. Like the murmuring inside a sea shell, she heard Darren's thin wailing, Stephen's whimpering. Finally, Mandy left her sitting there, hands still gripping the wheel. She took both children and walked along the road to the nearest cottage to use a phone.

At some point Shaun and his Dad arrived, looming grey and ghostly out of the darkness. Shaun, a tall, thin young man with a narrow and unshaven face and the sad, tensed lips of a disillusioned child, silently unloaded the shopping and put Mandy and the children into the garage truck. Douglas Evans murmured soothing inconsequential words, talked to Alex about the weather and tomorrow's football match in the next village and told her all about her new battery, just delivered, which he would fit as soon as she could pop into the garage. He gently but firmly eased Alex's hands from the steering-wheel and persuaded her to slide over into the passenger seat.

'Fetch her friend, Helen Andrews. She'll take care of her', said Mandy. 'I have to get the kids home to bed.'

So Douglas drove her back to the cottage, pausing *en route* to collect Helen, and left after conferring with her in subdued tones on the doorstep. Now Helen, frowning, sat across the table, listening to Alex's account of the day and its climax, and the story of another day and another child and another car, attempting to unravel her friend's confused state.

'But, Helen, that's really why I didn't want her. That's why I was never completely sure about her when Peter was alive, and why finally I couldn't accept her even when she seemed all I had left. Peter was more willing. Perhaps because he was sort of adopted himself and it really worked for him. But I struggled because she wasn't perfect. I couldn't admit it, but I wanted my own perfect baby, like Mandy.'

Sitting across the kitchen table from her, Helen sighed again.

'I'm trying to understand, Alex. Really I am. But you're not making it easy for me. What do you mean by a perfect baby?'

'That's what I always wanted for me and Peter. A perfect baby to bring up, to love perfectly, to care for perfectly, to do all the right things for. The way . . . the way my own parents didn't, couldn't do for me.'

Helen smiled faintly.

'Is it a perfect baby you wanted? Or the chance to be the perfect mother? Let me tell you about Sarah. When she was born, I thought, "I have the perfect baby." She was gorgeous. Beautiful miniature fingers and toes and a few wisps of fluffy blonde hair. How we watched over that baby, doing everything just by the book! Feeds every four hours it was in those days, none of your demand feeding! I sterilized all the bottles just so and kept her immaculate.

'I remember the day we reached her first birthday. I remember thinking, "I've kept my perfect baby safe for one whole year." Then, the very next morning, she was tottering after me across the kitchen floor, made a grab for my skirt and missed. She fell hard on to the floor and caught her head on the cat's dish. I can still recall my absolute horror when I picked her up and saw the blood running down her face. Sarah still has that tiny scar, just above her right eye. I was absolutely distraught, condemning myself with the thought, "My baby isn't perfect any more." But, actually, I realized later that I was wrong. My baby had always been scarred.'

Alex stared at her, waiting, tears on her cheeks.

'In a way we're all scarred, aren't we? From the very beginning?' Helen went on.

'Take Sarah's sight. When I looked at my newborn baby's pale blue eyes I couldn't possibly know that she'd

175

inherited my bad sight. She's worn glasses since the age of five, poor kid. As a caring parent, it's hard not to feel guilt over things like that. And what other genetic imperfections are at work in her twenty-year-old body even now?'

She paused and frowned.

'That kind of scarring, I've really no control over. We none of us have, though I suppose in a funny sort of way we are indirectly responsible. But what about the emotional scarring I've been the cause of in Sarah's life? The things I really must take responsibility for because I could have controlled them? What about the times I was over-hasty, shouted at her, slapped her out of anger or frustration? What about the times I belittled her with words, undermined her confidence with my sarcasm? And how much, may God have mercy on us, have Trevor and I scarred her with the divorce?'

Helen bowed her head, rubbing her chin against her clasped hands.

'Are you with me, Alex? This little girl you've been telling me about tonight . . . Well, so she's got Down's syndrome. And a few other obvious problems. But what I'm trying to tell you is that in the end she may be less scarred than Sarah, or hundreds of other apparently perfect children. Believe me, as a teacher I've seen lots of children hurting in ways that wouldn't show up on a medical report. The scarring that shows isn't all the scarring there is. Can't you see that?'

Alex nodded slowly.

'I walked out on her, Helen. I've never seen it before, or perhaps I haven't faced up to it. But I turned my back and walked out on Siu Ling. Just like my mother walked out on me. You know, I don't think I've ever been able to forgive my mother for that one act, of walking away from me and my sisters. I realize I'm not a forgiving kind of person. But I've done the same thing. And perhaps with less reason. It all makes me a hypocrite of the very worst kind.'

'No, I wouldn't go that far. Don't punish yourself so much, dear. Even doctors don't like taking medicine. You wouldn't be the first person, or the last, to slip up on practising what you'd been preaching.'

'Since losing Peter, somehow I've been so scared of closeness, of any kind of intimacy. Even intimacy with God. Oh, everything's still raw, bleeding. I want to know the love of God like I used to, more than I used to. But I'm scared of being overwhelmed by it. Or maybe it's worse than that. I'm scared of finding it not enough.'

'I don't believe you'll be disappointed,' said Helen, softly. 'But you need to make a move. Do something to break up the emotional log-jam.'

'I know you're right. I'm just . . . not ready . . . not yet.'

'Alex, how long can you put it off? I don't want to push you. But you don't need to wait till you're ready. Maybe you'll never be ready, on your terms. Just as you are is fine for God.'

'Yes, I know, really. But I'm frightened.'

'No need. It's your Father we're talking about. Not a stranger. Or a judge.'

'Carry on. You're right. I need you to tell me all that and I need you to be hard on me. Thank you for being a true friend. But I don't know how to begin.'

Helen hesitated. 'I don't really know *how* you begin, either. Only you can decide that. But I wonder if the *where* might help.'

Looking around the kitchen, she stood to her feet.

'This place. Perhaps it's too full of memories and broken

dreams. Come on. I've got the church keys. I'll drive you. Put something warm on. I doubt whether the heating will be on, this time of night.'

'*Come, let us reason together, says the Lord.*'

'What?'

'I think it's in Isaiah. It's just come into my mind. You're right, Helen. I need to work things out with God, to reason with him, and can't afford to put it off any longer.'

The decision made her feel nervous, like a girl on a first date.

But after all, St Matthew's was neither locked nor empty.

As Helen parked up against the railings, a few warm jewels of colours spilled out over the churchyard. They glanced up at the shepherd with a lamb around his shoulders staring down at them from the lit east window.

'Sorry. Perhaps it won't be easy to have some quiet contemplation here tonight.'

Three men were manhandling a huge fir tree through the church porch. A fourth was walking slowly up the churchyard path through the gloom with both arms clasped around a huge plastic sack. He stopped when he saw Helen and lowered his head.

'Mrs Andrews?'

'Is that you, George?'

'Yes. Me and the others are setting up the Christmas tree in the church tonight. The missus and some volunteers from the youth club's coming round tomorrow to decorate it.'

He grunted as he lifted the sack again.

Helen handed Alex a large key.

'I'll let them know you'll turn out the lights and lock up

178

behind you,' she whispered. 'Or would you like me to come back for you, in an hour or so?'

'No. That's all right. I'll walk back. The rain's gone off now.'

Helen searched the sky.

'Yes. It's going to be a clear night. I can already see one or two stars.'

She briefly clasped Alex in her arms.

'Good night, dear. I'll give you a call in the morning. Or you call me, if you need me. Any time.'

Inside, the smell of pine resin was almost intoxicating. Alex slid into a pew about halfway down the church. Helen spoke briefly to the four men and indicated in her direction. They nodded. Helen waved and disappeared through the porch.

One of the men laughed out loud.

'Here, George, your good lady'll be after us, won't she! We laid a trail of pine needles right up the aisle.'

'Aah, she won't mind. She's a good sort, my missus. Can't make an omelette without breakin' eggs. I'll be sure to tell her she needs to get the broom out tomorrow.'

With an excess of panting and good-natured joking, the tree was slowly eased into an upright position and planted into a barrel of sand.

'It's a fair size this year. I reckon it's a good fifteen foot if it's an inch!'

At Stonebridge Road, the three-foot plastic conifer had wobbled precariously on its plastic tripod.

'Watch out! Don't be so clumsy. You'll have the whole thing over in a minute. You finished with the paper chains? Now, hang on. I'll just plug the lights in.'

Two dozen pinpoints of lights danced, magically transforming the tree.

179

'Smashing! Yer mother'll love that, won't she?'

'But, Dad . . .'

'An' I got her favourites. See here? Ready to go under the tree. Pound of raspberry ruffles.' There was a note of triumph in his voice.

Christmas Eve. Three months, one week and four days since Lizzie Travers had walked out into the night.

'Now, have you put that chicken on the draining-board and mixed up the sage and onion yet? Right then, you get off to bed, my girl. I jus' got to wrap up they dollies for Annie and young Lizzie.'

He was whistling as she wearily climbed the stairs. She knew he would leave the front door unbolted again tonight. She anticipated the truth, that the morning would dawn cheerless and he would appear grey-faced and blank-eyed, hope dwindling. Surely Christmas would beckon her back?

She did not reappear. Not for another two months, when news came that she had been found floating, nudging the weeds at the river edge, face down. She was wearing entirely different clothes, but there was no doubt it was her.

'Funny,' said Dad. 'They showed me a red cardigan. Yer mother never wore red. Never. Cheap. She said it made 'er look cheap.'

Foul play not suspected. Dad silently bolted the door every night after that.

The mystery of the missing five months was never solved. How could someone disappear like that, without a trace?

Over the years, Alex had fabricated a dozen possible one-act plays. Her child's eye saw her mother roaming the countryside with a band of gypsies, by night crouching

180

over a camp fire in her Paisley headscarf, by day selling pegs and sprigs of lucky heather door to door. Or she had joined a circus, and sewed spangles on tunics for bareback riders. As the years went by, the scenes grew less fanciful, more coarse. She ran off with an insurance salesman who soon tired of her. She lost her memory and lived in a squat with down and outs. She spent her days sitting in public libraries and her nights shivering in the bus station, scavenging for spilt food in bins at the back doors of restaurants. In her mid teens Alex was tormented that she'd not herself searched the libraries during that five months, not visited the bus stations, rail stations, soup kitchens, hostels. 'But they looked,' Dad assured her, with some impatience. 'You gotta hand it to 'em. They police was damn good. Looked everywhere. It was in all the papers, love.'

And then with the passage of years came the anger. Incomprehensible that a mother should leave her children. Unnatural. It was an act of cowardice and betrayal.

There was a dull thud as the heavy church door closed behind the men. The tall fir tree stood firm, proud, rich green, still more living than dead, rain droplets gleaming here and there on the heavy branches.

'Jehovah Shammah, the Lord who is there, forgive me for not forgiving my mother . . .'

So began the list, the private litany.

She searched her heart, scoured it till it bled, unearthed accusations held on to stubbornly for so long.

'Help me to understand . . .'

She needed to see from different angles, like Mandy needed to look afresh at her young husband's fascination with gambling. If Alex could find reasons for Shaun's addiction, empathize with his weakness, then surely for her own mother she could make reasonable excuse? And so, kneeling there in the silent church, she walked in her mother's shoes for a while, suffered alongside her through the stigma of a youthful pregnancy caused by ignorance, struggled in the daily battle of living with a man who was feckless and weak and changeable as the weather, felt the weight of not being able to provide for the four daughters to whom she gave life.

Soon Alex felt she had a glimpse of her distress. And Lizzie Travers had no God to turn to. No refuge earthly or eternal. So she cast away her life, believing it useless, and believing that the years had nothing to offer but more shame and more disappointment. People underestimate disappointment. Perhaps that's what was meant by dying of a broken heart.

Her father she was also determined to lay to rest. His faults she was intimate with, but what of his heartaches? Alex accused herself of lack of love, that the faith she herself had found had never extended hope or help to him, but only raised another wall between them.

Alex felt afresh the starkness of one particular truth she always tried to avoid, that her family had not seen in her enough Christlikeness to draw even one of them to faith. It had merely set her more apart.

She felt the shadows of the past rising up to meet her from the grey flagstones of the church floor. She resisted the urge to run but held herself on her knees in the lonely polished pew as she struggled to recognize the spectres, to name them and then to face them. She put herself on trial for her hardness of heart and knew she had already served most of the sentence inside the prison wall she had built for herself. She raised a hammer to the wall and chipped away at its substance. Newer bricks tumbled with a little effort of realization, but ancient stones resisted the blows, and began to disintegrate only under tears.

But the last release was the sweetest.

'And, Peter, I forgive you, my always love, for leaving me behind.'

POSTSCRIPT

The pale grey February light slanting through the bedroom window threw diamonds on to the new turquoise carpet scattered with Lego bricks. Alex rested her hand on the wall, invoking the name of Jehovah Rapha, the Lord who heals, to be present in the room. The wall was an inviting fresh lemon colour that made her think of eggs and butter and home baking. She admired the paper frieze of excited open-billed ducks eternally tumbling around the walls at shoulder height, stroked the yellow duvet covers on the pine bunks.

'Mandy, you've made a really super job of this!' she called out. 'The boys must love it!'

'They do. And I'm really pleased with it myself,' confessed Mandy, peering round the door, wiping her hands on her apron.

She laughed. 'I've never tried anything like this before, but it's come out well. Shaun says I must have an artistic streak we never knew about. I've got all sorts of plans for our bedroom, too.'

'Promise me you'll write and tell me all about it?'

'Of course. If you'll not mind the spelling mistakes!'

'And I shall want to know straight away, in May, when . . .'

'You'll be one of the first to know,' said Mandy, stroking her plump stomach. 'Promise. You be sure to send us a note of your new address and telephone number, as soon as you're settled.

'Well,' she added, a little nervously, 'you just take your time having a last look round. I'll be in the kitchen. Tea without milk, you said?'

She disappeared along the landing. Alex glanced up at the loft door and thought of the neat row of boxes. She felt peaceful about leaving everything. It was all in safe hands. And by that, she didn't mean Shaun and Mandy. She was learning to hold the past more lightly, and to reach for the future with a new courage.

And as for the present? The nightmare still returned occasionally, still vivid and awful, reducing her to trembling and tears. Her heart still ached sorely for her loss. But the sorrow was more gentle, less traumatic. There was no forgetting. Indeed, she wanted none. But the forgiving had set in motion the healing that she longed for. And she now had the will to seek to repair what was still redeemable. That's why she was going back. Because there were things unresolved that she no longer had to run from, even though she didn't understand how history would unfold, or how things broken could easily be made whole. But she was willing, with the God who was there and who was both healer and redeemer, to go back and pick up the pieces.

She found Mandy pouring tea at the kitchen table.

'This house is going to be a real blessing to you. You

don't know how happy this makes me feel,' said Alex, half to herself.

'It's all thanks to you,' said Mandy, pink creeping over her freckled cheeks. 'Some days I think I'm dreaming. I think I'm going to wake up back in Swan Court. I can't believe how good you've been to us, giving us this chance to start again, this lovely cottage virtually rent-free, the money for the decorating materials . . .'

'Thank God, Mandy, thank God. Remember, he's the one who really gives us second chances. We can only share what he's first given us. I shan't need the cottage for the next couple of years. Maybe longer. God's giving me a fresh start, too.'

Alex tapped her handbag.

'It's all there. Passport and ticket. It's good of Douglas to drive me to the airport this afternoon. We've only got to pick up my bags from Helen's. I'm all packed.'

'And you say someone's meeting you at the other end?'

'Oh, yes. Sister Bridget will be there. And someone else. Someone very special.'